"You didn't believe Willy Brown, did you?" I asked the guard as he closed the door behind us.

"Let me put it this way. Practically every inmate has a story how he was framed—and most of them sound a lot better than this one."

"But it could be true?"

"Maybe, but what can you do?"

The farther I walked away from that holding cell and the courthouse, the more I realized that I didn't have to think that there was nothing I could do.

Not yet.

LARRY WEINBERG is the author of several books for young adults. He lives in Woodstock, New York.

THE BIG STORY

Larry Weinberg

Pacer BOOKS FOR YOUNG ADULTS

BERKLEY BOOKS, NEW YORK

THE BIG STORY

A Berkley/Pacer Book, published by arrangement
with the author

PRINTING HISTORY
Berkley/Pacer edition/August 1986

ISBN: 0-425-08888-X
RL: 5.2

Pacer is a trademark belonging to
The Putnam Publishing Group.

A BERKLEY BOOK® TM 757,375
Berkley/Pacer Books are published by The Berkley Publishing Group,
200 Madison Avenue, New York, NY 10016.
The name "BERKLEY" and the stylized "B" with design are
trademarks belonging to the Berkley Publishing Corporation.

PRINTED IN THE UNITED STATES OF AMERICA

Chapter 1

IN MY IMAGINARY life I was already the famous Caroline Burns, whom television viewers saw every night reporting from the battle lines of Beirut, the twisting streets of Cairo, Peking's Forbidden City, the rain forests of Macao. But in the real world I was only a reporter for my high school paper covering the latest student council meeting—or, if I was lucky, the scandal of the missing gym shoes. Well, I was working hard for Capital High's *Speaking Out*, but I knew that if I ever wanted to lead the life I dreamed, I couldn't just watch the water pass through my toes as it drained out of the bathtub—which was what I was doing at the moment. I guess I somehow saw that water as symbolizing my promising future emptying itself down the drain.

"Caroline, it's time for some action!" I told myself. And that's when I immediately forgot my fear of rejec-

tion and decided to write a letter to the one person I
thought might ever possibly be willing to help me.

I jumped out of the tub, wrapped myself in a towel,
and found the pen and pad I usually reserved for real
hot stories for the school paper.

Dear Ms. Richie:

I admire you very much, both as a newscaster and
as a human being who is warm, sincere and always
concerned about the welfare of people. Your caring
spirit comes through no matter what you are reporting on the evening news—and I suppose that is
what makes the difference between you and so
many others who simply seem to be saying the
words.

As a reporter for *Speaking Out*, which you yourself started when you were a student at Capital
High ten years ago, I have been watching your
career for some time. I have to say that you are the
reason I decided when I was fourteen years old that
I wanted to become a television journalist. Please
don't think that I am gushing, but you inspired me
then, and now I watch your program every night to
learn from you.

Now comes the part I'm afraid to bring up,
because you are going to be much too busy! Would
it be possible for me to interview you for a feature
article? I'm sure that the students would love to
read about you. It will not only be a great honor for
me, but—to be honest—it will also give me a
chance to ask questions that I ardently hope will
help me follow in your footsteps. (And I know you
are destined for much greater things!)

I'm sorry, but now I'm going to add pushiness to gushiness and ask you to please let me know soon, since I would like to get this article in print before summer vacation.

Very Sincerely Yours,
Caroline Burns

Barbara Richie was a co-anchor at the local television station, and I honestly meant every word I had said in my letter; she was my inspiration. I just knew she was to go right to the top! Plus I hoped that writing to her would help me break some ground for my future.

I didn't even wait to redo the letter in the typewriter. I knew that if I did, I'd find I didn't like the letter. Then I'd rewrite this and rewrite that—and it would *never* get out. So I threw on a robe and ran out across the lawn, barefoot, to the corner mailbox, and plopped it in.

I won't drag things out. Obviously, if I never heard from Barbara Richie, I wouldn't have a story to tell. What happened was that when a week went by with no answer at all, I figured that was the end of it. My mother, who always believed that everything important to a person tends to move toward you like a glacier, just a few inches a century, told me not to "jump to conclusions"—which I did anyway. But in the middle of the next week, there it was—a note from Barbara Richie—and handwritten like my own!

Dear Caroline,

Thank you for your letter. I admire your direct-ness and ambition. I don't know what it is I am "destined for," but if you can come to the station next Monday afternoon at 3:30, I will be glad to give you the interview.

B.R.

Chapter 2

GETTING FROM SCHOOL to Channel 12 on Monday was an adventure in itself. My friend Helen was only one week into her driver's license, and getting her parents' permission to use the car was like pulling teeth. She was a year older than I, but even so it was absolutely amazing that they ever let her make the trip alone through downtown traffic, or that she was willing to do it. As it was, the engine ran on a mixture of gasoline and hysteria, especially when the other drivers began to rain angry stares and horn honks down on us for reasons neither of us could possibly understand. Still and all, we made it to the station with no major dents—and only five minutes late for my interview.

We had pulled in behind the station near a very large van that had a big antenna on the roof and the words WKNR Mobile Unit painted on its side. The motor was idling, and as I started to walk across the parking lot, two men hurried out of a side door of the television station, heading for the van. One of them balanced a video camera on his right shoulder and a piece of equipment slung by a strap from the other.

"Excuse me," I sort of blurted as they swept past. "Is that the entrance to the news department?"

"Who are you looking for?" asked the cameraman, who kept on walking, only backward now, as he turned to me.

"Barbara Richie. I've got an appointment."

"Barb's on special assignment at city hall," the other man cut in impatiently as he opened the passenger door of the big van. "Let's move it or that factory will burn down before we get there. If Channel 8 beats me to the only good eyewitness, Paul will have a nervous break-down."

"Coming, Mother!" The cameraman swung away from me, jumped in behind the wheel, and the van started to move.

"Do you know when she'll be back?" I called after them. But the van zoomed away, leaving me alone in the parking lot. Figuring the door they had come out of was the entrance to the newsroom, I simply went in.

I walked straight into a madhouse—at least that's how it seemed for the first couple of seconds. Someone was shouting. There were two television sets high up on the far wall playing soap operas from two different stations at the same time. From another corner of the place, there came what sounded like a bunch of police and fire radios, all going at once, with people talking over static.

The shouting voice belonged to a small, balding, scowling man just ahead of me in the room, which was filled with a ton of desks and typewriters. He was standing behind a counter and in front of a huge blackboard with writing all over it, bellowing at someone who was walking out of the room. Racing would be more like it.

At the very moment that I decided to look for someone else to speak to, his eyes zeroed in on me. He gave me a long stare, then tossed away the wet, unlit cigarette that had been dangling Bogart-style from his mouth, and calmly said at last, "And what, may I ask, do you want?"

"I . . . uh . . . have an appointment with Ms. Richie. My name's Caroline Burns. I'm doing an interview for my school—"

He cut me off. "Reception let you through just like that?"

The question must have given me a flustered look because he proceeded to explain in a tone that assumed I was a two-year-old: "There's a desk up in the front of the building. That's where you have to go and check in when you come to meet someone. Then the receptionist tells us all about it."

I started to say "sorry," when he looked away from me and turned his attention to one of those little police radios. I moved in close and saw that they were set up in a row behind the counter where his desk was. A voice came through the static and I made out something about a "car 21" reporting and that there was a number something or other "in progress at the Shop-Rite supermarket in the Westbrook Mall."

"Terrific!" the man cried out in a loud complaint. "An armed robbery! Police have 'em cornered—and I have nobody to send without pulling somebody off of something else!''

"Blake ought to be finishing his story by now," said a younger, black man, who was glancing up at the big board. "Maybe you'll catch him in his car, Paul."

Paul sat down quickly. And as I moved in a little closer to see what he was doing, he snapped a little plastic microphone off his desk.

"Blake? Hey, Blake? Are you there—or taking in a movie?"

"Here," the voice of Barbara's co-anchorperson came back.

"Don't talk. Listen! Shop-Rite market, Westbrook Mall. Robbers cornered. Tell that cameraman of yours to show a little hustle. If there's action, I want pix!"

"Lone Ranger and Tonto are on our way!"

Paul grunted, then put down the mike and gazed at me. "Look around at what's happening here. We've got ratings sweeps going on now and no one has time to catch their breath. Do you really think Barbara can take the time to be interviewed today—or any time in the next week or so?"

"I . . . guess not."

"Okay. I'll let her know you were here. She'll be in touch."

I can't tell you how depressed I suddenly became. Nodding, I shuffled to the door.

Just as I got there, it swung open and a beautiful woman with almond-shaped eyes and raven black hair blazed past me. In the state I was in, I was halfway through the door before I realized that the person who had gone by was Barbara Richie herself.

I turned back into the newsroom and saw her already talking to Paul.

"Where's your cameraman?" Paul was asking.

"Don'll be along in a moment. He can edit the shots for me. He knows what I want. Anyway, I wrote up the script for this package during the drive back."

"Let's see." He reached for the notebook in her hand.

They stopped talking for a moment while he read. This is my chance! I told myself. But still I didn't move. I just couldn't bring myself to walk back across the newsroom.

"Looks like the same old stuff," Paul said, handing it back to her. "The mayor has stalled you again."

"Only in words," she grinned. "Wait until you see him breaking out in a hot political sweat all over the footage."

"*Now* you're talking."

I stood there working up the nerve to call out to her. In fact, my mouth was just about open when Paul's eyes landed on me once more. There were no words, but his stare said it all. My courage went down into my shoes. I gave up and, pushing out into the parking lot, let the door close behind me.

All I wanted now was to get away as quickly as I could. Crossing to where we had parked, I rapped on the window of the car for Helen to unlock my door.

"What's wrong with you?" she asked, letting me in. I guess she saw the look on my face and that I was fighting off tears. "Hey, what happened?"

"Can't we just go?"

As she reached out to turn the ignition key, Helen must have glanced up into the rearview mirror. Suddenly she gave a little gasp, fell against the back of her seat, and began sliding downwards to the floor. That's when I heard a woman's voice calling, "Caroline?"

Turning, I saw Barbara Richie. She was hurrying toward the car! She leaned her head in my window with a big, bright, cheerful smile. "Where are you going? I thought we had a date for an interview?"

"But . . . uh . . . I was told you were too busy."

"I sure am!" she laughed. "Much too busy! Most people you want to interview are too busy or annoyed—or too something. But a good reporter doesn't let anything keep her from a story! Now don't let Paul Morris or anybody else prevent you from doing your job."

She stared past me at Helen. "Hello down there—I'm Barbara Richie."

" 'Lo," came an almost inaudible answer.

"This is my best friend, Helen," I said. "Sometimes she's a little shy. . . ."

"I certainly know that feeling," said Ms. Richie, extending her hand to Helen.

It seemed to be a standoff, because Helen didn't move and Barbara didn't pull her hand back. But finally Helen sat up and took it. "Pleased to meet you," she said with just the beginning of a little grin.

"Same here—and call me Barbara. Are you coming inside with us?"

"Oh, no!" Helen was ready to collapse again.

"Well, see you later then. Come on, Caroline." She opened the car door, slipped her arm under mine, and together we sailed back into the newsroom.

Chapter 3

PAUL MORRIS GAVE US a disgruntled look as we entered. "There's a lot to do between now and the broadcast, Barbara," he warned as softly as he could.

"O, ye of little faith!" she sang back at him in a playful soprano, meanwhile maneuvering me across the newsroom to one of the many doors. Shutting the door behind us, she waved me to one of the chairs in front of a mirror that crossed an entire wall and had dozens of tiny white light bulbs spread in a row along the top of it. It surprised me; somehow I only expected to see this kind of dressing room in the backstage of a theater.

"Usually," she said, "I get into my makeup just before we set up for the broadcast, but this will give us a breather to talk."

Undoing a few hairpins in front of the mirror, she broke into another smile. "Okay, what would you like to know?"

"Uh . . . how did you get started?"

"Well, after I left good old Capital High . . . How is it, by the way?"

"All right." I gave her a little shrug. "Actually sort of boring."

"Don't I know what you mean. And the food?"

"*Terrible!*"

"Is it? We ran a whole campaign in *Speaking Out* to change that ten years ago."

"We still are."

"Well, you'll be sorry to hear that college food isn't always much better. But that's where I got my first on-the-air experience—working at the radio station run by the university. Also I wrote a sports column for the school paper there. They didn't want to give it to me, of course. But I pestered them into it."

She broke into a big laugh. "Had to secretly teach myself what those football games were all about first! . . . A local TV station became intrigued with the idea of a female sportscaster—that was a new gimmick then— which, to tell the truth, is why I got into it. They gave me a job when I got out of college, and I convinced them to let me cover the rest of the news."

"Sounds like you really have to keep after people," I said.

"But *charmingly*, Caroline. Always charmingly."

I thought I might as well get to the questions *I* was here to ask. The ones for the paper could wait. "I . . . was wondering if a person *always* has to wait until they go through four years of college. Wouldn't they hire you otherwise? I mean, can't you get the experience some other way?"

She leaned back in her chair and gave me a long look.

"Why is it I get the impression, Caroline, that you're a bit impatient? You want to get started right away, huh? Big dreams? Visions of yourself reporting from all over the world?"

"Well . . . yes. It's just that I know what I want to do and I don't want to wait."

She lifted an eyebrow. "Well, Caroline, I must tell you you've got a lot to learn before you get started in this business. Four years of college or not." Just then there was a knock on the door. "Yes?"

"Barbara"—it was a woman's voice—"Mr. Hammersmith and Mr. Meyers want to see you upstairs." She made a big deal about the word *upstairs* as if that meant the height of something.

"Can't it wait a few more minutes?"

"It's about your contract and the offer."

Barbara jumped up from her chair. Interview over. "Caroline, I'm sorry, but I have to go now."

"That's okay." What else could I say? I hadn't gotten a chance to ask too many questions. I was frustrated by the way everything had come to an end so suddenly. "What kind of offer is it?" I asked as she headed for the door.

She turned to me with her hand on the knob and smiled. "Strictly off the record?"

I nodded.

"The major leagues want me."

"Major leagues?"

"This is only a local station, Caroline. I only broadcast news in this area. The new job will have me on the air from coast to coast."

"That's—that's fabulous! Congratulations!" I was

ecstatic. It was as if it was all happening to me at the same time as her.

"Yes," she said, drawing away, "but keep your fingers crossed for me. I still have a little legal problem." She lowered her voice. "They have to let me out of my contract here, which has two more years to run. And that's what this meeting is about."

"Good luck!"

She turned around in the doorway. "Send me a copy of your article. I'm dying to read it."

"I will, I will," I promised.

"She's wonderful, isn't she?" said Helen when I got back into the car.

"She sure is."

I went on and on about Barbara Richie on the way home. Then I ran inside to get my article written while our conversation was still fresh in my mind. Well, of course I wrote about the things we had talked of—some of them. But also about the kind of person she was, so full of energy and fun and concern—so interested in helping a person she'd never even seen before.

The issue came out about a week later—and I sent a copy to her at the station, along with a little note hoping that her "legal problem" had come around right.

Exactly on my birthday—like the best present I ever had—a letter came in the mail. It was typewritten and from the assistant manager of the station.

Dear Miss Burns,

We are writing to ask if you would be interested in serving an internship in our newsroom during the first month of your summer vacation. The job is purely voluntary and without pay, but it will give you the opportunity to learn firsthand about the daily work of broadcast journalism. Ordinarily our station's internship program is made available only to journalism students currently attending an accredited college or university. But Miss Richie has convinced us to make an exception in your case.

Please advise of your acceptance by mail or telephone to the undersigned at this office.

At the bottom was a little penned-in note:

Dear Caroline,
Congratulations! How about we get *you* started? Concerning that "problem"—I'm still working on it. Look forward to seeing you.

                                    Barbara.

P.S. It was a wonderful article.

Chapter 4

I HAD MADE up my mind not to let Paul Morris and his scowl ruin what was going to be a wonderful experience in my life. So the moment I walked into that newsroom several weeks later I headed straight for the assignment desk with my prepared speech about how I intended to work just as hard and well as any college student he could find.

Maybe it was the look in my eye that caused him to cut me off before I began. "How about some coffee?"

"Uh, sure . . . no sugar." The truth was I didn't even like coffee, but if this was a peace gesture, I was going to go along with it.

"Okay," he said, walking to a coffee machine on a stand near the teletypes. "Hang your raincoat in the closet over there."

He handed me a full, styrofoam cup when I returned to the desk.

"Thank you, Mr. Morris."

"Paul's okay. Come around on this side of the counter and sit down."

There was a little desk—really a table with a typewriter and phone on it—near his own desk, and I sat down at it.

"Here's the score." He took a sip of his coffee, swiveled around in his chair, and looked at me as if for the first time. "I've got nothing personal against you. You're wrong if you think so. But—number one—four weeks in my book isn't enough to train anybody to do much of anything. Two—even if it was, I'm too busy for it. What you pick up you'll have to do on your own. Three—don't touch any equipment without my permission—or do anything else without it. Four—time is short around this place. Remember that you're here to work. This isn't fun and games."

He held up his hand to cut me off before I reacted. "No offense. Just laying out the rules of the road." Meanwhile he'd been gathering some papers together as if he were about to get up. "Well, kid, that's about it. I gotta go."

"If you don't mind," I said sternly, "I think I'd like to be called by my own name—Caroline."

"Suit yourself," he shrugged, standing up. Then he turned to a nearby cubbyhole. "Bill, have you checked out the wire services for anything we could put in the line-up?"

The young black man who had been working with him during my last visit looked up from a nearby file cabinet. "Yeah. You want me to go over it with you before you go inside to see Dave?"

"No, come on in with me; the kid—I mean Caroline here'll handle the desk."

"Wait—" I said, feeling a rising panic as I looked around at all the radios and other stuff. "What do you want me to do?"

"Show her, Bill, then come on inside. And bring any updates on events happening today I don't know about."

"You've got 'em all except for that big organ being put in that church in Guilderstern."

"I can live without it." And he went through a door.

"Okay, now let me tell you what to do," Bill began. "These fire and police scanners work by themselves, see? Don't change anything. You hear a call that sounds right for us, jot down where and what, then run like a beaver to get Paul—so he or I can come back and dispatch a reporting team to cover it while it's still warm. What we're always looking for is something dramatic—and hopefully something you can shoot some footage on."

"But how do I know what's what? They use those numbers to describe what's going on, don't they?"

"Not always, but here's this list." He pulled a sheet of paper from a drawer. "Sit over here and answer any phone calls, too. It's a matter of judgment whether to interrupt us or not. And always get a name and a call-back number. Gotta go."

"Can you tell me what a line-up is?" I called as he started across the room.

"It's what goes on first, second, and like that over the six o'clock broadcast. What we're gonna cover."

His hand was already on the doorknob, but I was in this job to learn. "Isn't it too early to be doing that?

Won't there be a lot of other things happening in the news between now and broadcast time?''

"We keep changing it, but this gives us something to shoot at." He pushed the door open.

"Who's Dave?"

Bill stopped—and looked a little exasperated.

"Dave Hammersmith is the Boss of All Bosses in the newsroom. The news manager." And with that he disappeared.

So I sat at Paul Morris's desk waiting for something to happen, but kind of hoping nothing would. And for a while nothing did, except that there were a couple of calls for reporters and photographers who weren't there. Then suddenly one of the police scanners crackled. A very urgent-sounding voice cried out that a "two-fourteen" was going on, and one of the patrol cars was ordered to answer it right away. I quickly ran down my list but couldn't even find that number on the page. My first thought was that in spite of how it sounded, this couldn't have been an important crime since it wasn't even on Paul's list. But then I thought: hey, maybe this is just a rare one. Or maybe this list is incomplete. Or maybe this isn't on the list because everybody *knows* what it is!

Now what? I didn't want to make a fool of myself by bothering them for nothing. But then I didn't want to risk overlooking something important, either. I got up and went into the room of the Boss of All Bosses.

I found the three men seated around a conference table. This Dave, a slightly paunchy man with a soft, cream cheese face, was pointing with his pipe as I stepped inside. "I don't know if I go along with you,

Paul. I agree that it's a local story with a national angle, but I don't see it as the lead one.''

"I just have the feeling something could happen when General Wassly comes in at the airport. So does Blake. He's dying to cover the general's arrival. Thinks the network will pick it up.''

"Excuse me," I said. Paul looked up at me. "I'm sorry to interrupt you, but there's a 214.''

"A which?" Bill asked.

"On the police radio.''

"Forget *that* one," Bill grinned, and there was a burst of laughter. I felt ridiculous, but I didn't even know why.

"Who is this young lady?" asked the man behind the pipe smoke.

"Caroline Burns," Paul answered. "Our new intern.''

"Oh yes, the high school student. Paul, why don't you explain to her what a 214 is?''

"It's one of the special numbers they've made up to signal each other. This one's to warn some cop to stay away from the station house for one reason or another. Like maybe somebody he owes money to has shown up. They've got private signals for all kinds of things. You didn't do anything wrong. Go back.''

Bill got up. "I'll go cover the desk now. I've got something to run down anyway." He headed for the door.

"Let's ask what she thinks about the issue," Dave Hammersmith said after Bill had left the room. "How much interest do you think the public has in something to do with a war that was over so long ago?''

"Do you mean Vietnam?''

"Yes.''

"Well, I think there's plenty of interest," I said. "A lot of kids my age wonder about it."

"Yes, but is it news?"

"I'm . . . not sure I understand what you mean."

"Current. Worth covering."

Paul jumped in before I could answer. "Agent Orange *is* worth covering, Dave, because these men are suffering from the effects of it right now. And they hold Wassly responsible for giving the orders that exposed them to it. They figure he knew what it could do—and he probably did know. Besides, we could be awfully sorry if we don't get a crew out to the airport and Channel 8 does."

The news manager, having forgotten all about my opinion, blew a long column of smoke while he thought it over. "All right. But give the story to Barbara, not Blake."

"Hey, come on Dave, be fair. Blake has the experience. He covered Vietnam for years—and everything to do with it. And the public identifies that kind of a story with a male personality."

"That's true. But he also doesn't hold on to the viewers as well as she does. You saw the report we got after the ratings. Besides, I've got to try to keep Barbara happy. You know what's going on with her. . . . She practically threw the raise in our faces. . . ."

"We got somebody listening to us here," Paul muttered, meaning me.

I took that as my cue to leave. "Well, thanks for setting me straight on the 214. I'll get back to the desk."

"Before you go," said the news manager, "would

you bring over the water pitcher and those glasses on that tray?"

"Sure."

"So what's next?" Dave went on as I turned toward the little stand the tray was resting on.

"Next," said Paul, "is they're picking a jury at the end of the week in the Willy Brown case."

Dave shrugged. "I don't see much to do with it until the trial starts."

Paul leaned forward. "I think it's a hot case right now."

"Hot? Why?" asked Dave, taking a long pull on his pipe. "It looks like an open-and-shut murder case to me."

Murder—this sounded interesting and I didn't want to leave just yet. So I started *serving* the water. After all, I thought, who could object to that?

"Look," Paul continued, "you've got a black migrant worker from the South with no money and no clout living in some shack he doesn't even own—and the victim's a wealthy farmer's wife whose husband is also a big political leader. It's got contrast coming out of the ears. We could do a real background build-up on both the murdered woman and the accused. It would really hype our coverage when the trial starts."

Dave tipped his chair back and stared at the ceiling. "I hear what you're saying, but I'm tired of us being rapped all the time for being too sensational."

Paul sounded amazed. "I don't get it. You're the one who's always saying news is also show biz. All this is is a little honest showmanship."

"Maybe, but drop it for now."

It was at this point that Paul looked at my hand as I

slowly set a glass of water down in front of him. His eyes traveled back up my arm and came to a hard stop at my face. "I thought you were headed for the desk. Something wrong?"

"No . . ."

"Then what are you doing here?"

"Well . . . I . . ."

"Don't be hard on her," said his boss. "She's only an intern." And he smiled at me.

I can tell you right now I liked Paul's scowl a lot better than his boss's condescending smile.

I kind of smiled back at him and then dashed out of the room and straight into someone standing right outside the door. I knocked him backwards.

"Careful!" he shouted, trying to save his bobbing camera from falling.

"Oh, I'm sorry!"

"Ah, you do move swiftly," the man declared in a British accent. He grinned at me.

"I wish you'd tell that to Paul," I said, trying at least not to *sound* like a clown.

"Aha! Now I know who you are." He stuck out his left hand for me to shake—the big video camera was in his right. "Welcome. I'm Don LeFever, Barbara's eyes. Where is she?"

"I haven't seen her," I replied, and was about to thank him for his welcome when he turned to Bill, who was seated at his desk.

"She didn't come in?"

Bill shook his head.

"Did she call?"

"Nope."

"I'll be damned. Maybe she meant it."

"Meant what?" Bill asked with a worried look as he crossed to the big counter where the scanners were going.

"I'm not saying, mate. I'm out of it. Got to go pre-edit what I shot on the highway."

I felt a light breeze as the side door to the newsroom opened behind me and I heard, "I'd appreciate it if everyone here stayed 'out of it.' My business is my business, thank you."

Chapter 5

I TURNED AROUND quickly. It was Barbara. She seemed very angry.

Paul came out of Dave's office just in time to hear her statement. He gave her a fixed look. "You're late—and why are you so testy?"

"I don't care if I'm late. And I'm not being testy."

"You look like hell. Didn't you get any sleep last night?" Paul asked.

"What I do at night is my business! You realize, don't you, that if I don't get my release from the contract this week, I'll lose my shot at the network. They'll take someone else!"

"Hey, this is a place where we work on the *news*, nothing else—and I'm not going to argue with you. This is not the time or place to start up with your contract, Barbara. You got less than an hour to go down

with Don to the airport. General Wassly is coming in
. . . the vets are up in arms . . .''

"That's Blake's turf, isn't it?"

"Dave wants me to give it to you."

"Why? So every night I can get more doses of jealousy
and hatred from the guy? I don't want to compete with
the man! In fact, I don't want this job—and I am
quitting!"

Up to this point I had just been a casual observer to
what was going on, but Barbara's announcement gave
me something of that same burn in my stomach I had
felt that night when my father came in and told us he
was leaving home. I know it sounds stupid to compare
them, but it's true. I wasn't any more concerned for
what she was going through than I had been for my
dad. All I could feel at that moment was the awful
sense of being deserted. I was glad when Paul said,
"Look, Barbara, you don't mean that."

"I do mean it. I'm going to tell what's-his-face right
now!"

Don had meanwhile come out of his editing room.
He and Paul dashed in front of her just as she lunged for
Hammersmith's office—and Paul caught her by the shoulders, pushing her back. "That's nuts! You'll only get
yourself blackballed up and down the line—and you
won't work anywhere."

"He's right, Barbara. It's the wrong move."

By now, other reporters and photographers were coming into the newsroom to get their assignments. Barbara
didn't seem to take any notice. "Why doesn't he come
out of his little nest!" she shouted at the door. "I know
he can hear me in there—the miserable coward! So the
management needs me two more years for its lousy

ratings? Tough! You know what you all can do with it!
I'm going back to newspapers!''

"No you aren't, kiddo!" exploded Paul, still holding
on to her. "You're going across the street with me to
the diner. We're gonna sit over coffee and talk about
what it means to be a *professional*—which is one of *your*
favorite topics!"

"Don't yell in my face!"

"Bill!" he barked over his shoulder, "get Blake on
the two-way and send him on the Wassly thing! He's
another prima donna. Where is he?"

"Don't know . . ."

"So you think I'm a prima donna?" Her eyes were
still smoldering.

"This time around, yeah."

"Anyone who calls me a name like that," she stormed,
"pays for the coffee."

"We'll see about that." And taking her by the arm,
he spun her around and led her out of the place.

The moment they were gone, there was a burst of
conversation. "Hey, Bill, what's coming off here? She
quitting?"

"Yeah, what gives?"

Bill shrugged. He obviously didn't want to get involved in any of this.

"Come on, boys, figure it out," said a man I recognized as one of the two sports announcers. "She's
going to make them so miserable, they'll have to let her
out of the contract."

"That isn't the way to go about getting what you
want *here*."

"It is when you've got no other choice."

The news manager put in a brief appearance now that

the coast was clear. "I would like to see this newsroom go back to acting like one," he said, making his point with a jab of his pipe. Then, shoving it back into his mouth, he returned to his office, closing the door behind him.

I waited around until Bill—who was assigning work in Paul's absence—finally looked up at me.

"Is there something I can do?" I asked.

He must have sensed how uncomfortable I was feeling.

"Caroline," he said softly, "here's where you start earning all that money we're not paying you. Have Don show you the footage he shot at the scene of the auto accident he just covered. Since there was no reporter with him, he's already got the stuff assembled in the right order to make a story out of it. So first ask him to run it all through for you. See if it's got any sound bites or talking heads in it."

"Excuse me?"

"Did he get anyone on his videotape talking to us? Telling us what was going on? I don't think he did. If not, just give me a one-minute narration, using this information we got from the highway patrol. Do you have a stopwatch?"

"No."

"Here's mine. When you write this, read it back aloud at the speed you think Barbara would do it. Only do it softly; there's enough noise around here. What I want is a ten-second lead-in where the viewers will see Barbara live, talking from the anchor desk. Then we go to the stuff Don shot—the cars and so on—with her still talking over it. Then we go from an ambulance at the scene, if there is one, to a hospital photograph we can pull out of records, and back to Barbara for a five second tag to close the story. If it looks good"—he smiled—"you may have something you wrote on the air tonight."

I was so thankful to Bill! He gave me the kind of challenge that I really needed to get my head out of a whirl—and I'm sure he knew it. I went in to see Don, who helped me a lot with suggestions. Then I found a desk no one was using at the moment and began to write. I think it took at least an hour to come up with a one-minute story that I felt good enough about to show to Bill.

"You've been doing some newspaper writing?" he asked after reading it over.

I took that for a compliment. "Yep."

"It shows. Reads very well—straight out of *The New York Times*. Now let's try saying it out loud, the way I advised you. 'An accident that narrowly averted tragic consequences occurred on the turnpike this morning when an automobile, being driven eastbound by an apparently intoxicated man from Sydenham, went out of control and, swerving across the center island—' "

"All right!" I cut in, embarrassed. "I get it."

"What?"

"Don't stuff all the information in the first sentence."

"For TV, you write the way people *talk*. Conversational. Give them just enough to hook them. Then spread out information . . . so you'll keep them interested all the way through. It's a *story*, got it?"

"I got it. It's so obvious, I don't know why I didn't realize it before."

"Who ever realizes the obvious? Here, try again."

So I slaved over it again. And this time I was *sure* I had gotten it right.

"Better," he said, "but now it's rambling. I'm no expert myself, but do you want me to show you how I would do it?"

"Don't you dare!"

"Okay then, give it another try."

I was still trying when Barbara and Paul got back. We all waited to see what kind of state she was in. There was no mystery about it—the blaze hadn't gone out of her eyes.

"Hammerhandle still in there?"

She was gazing straight past me, at Bill. He nodded yes.

She left Paul's side and bolted straight for the news manager's office. This time no one tried to stop her. "All right!" we heard her yell, "you guys win! I'm going to stay on and build your ratings and do a better job than ever before!"

Chapter 6

THINGS CALMED DOWN after that—for a newsroom. This, I was beginning to learn, is like saying the place went back to being a three-ring circus. Barbara got her way about not competing with her co-anchorperson on the General Wassly arrival, but only because a hot flash broke over fire and police scanners at the same time. Seconds later, a buzzer sounded on the Associated Press wire service machine. Paper started rolling out containing the bulletin that was automatically being printed out. Someone had started a fire that was threatening to destroy the National Guard arsenal twenty miles outside of town—and maybe a few acres of everything else nearby along with it.

"Take the remote van," Paul told Barbara and the cameraman. "I want go on the air with it, live, right away. You'll feed me the visuals from there as fast as you get them. Keep in touch—and don't get blown up."

"Don't worry, I've already blown up," she shot
back, and left.

Blake Thomas came in a little later. Nobody told him
about the quarrel. The smile left his face though, when
he heard about Barbara's rush assignment.

"What are you grousing about?" Paul muttered. "You
wanted to cover the general's arrival—and you got it.
Take it easy. You got a good one."

"Okay, okay. Can I take the remote van in case
there's big enough action at the airport to—"

"Barbara's got it."

"Barbara!"

"That's how it goes," the assignment editor sighed
as he stood up to stretch his legs. He lit a cigarette that
had been dangling all this time from his mouth. Then,
realizing he was smoking, he threw it away.

Blake Thomas turned around and stalked off. He
passed me on the way out, looking right through me as
if I wasn't there.

I went back to what I was doing and finished a
version of my story I thought Bill would finally accept.
I saw that he was busy with someone, so I left it on his
desk and went up to Paul.

"Anything else I can do?"

"Yeah—a favor." Reaching into his pocket he fished
out a few coins. "Here. Go down to the machines—
they're in a little room just behind reception—and
bring me back a pack of cigarettes."

Boy! I thought. Some assignment! All I said was,
"Which brand do you want?"

"Anything without filters. If I can't smoke it, at least
I want to taste it."

I thought of telling him that having a lot of tobacco

juice floating around in his mouth was probably not much better for him than smoking. But I decided he probably didn't want to hear that from me, so off I went. The only important knowledge I gained from *that* trip down three corridors was the location of the women's room.

When I came back, Paul grunted something that had to pass for a thank you, and I was left with nothing to do again. With the reporting teams gone, the newsroom was practically deserted. Bill picked up my work, studied it, then walked over to the assignment desk where I was still standing.

"Hey, Paul, this one can write. Her copy's pretty good. What do you think?" He handed over what I had typed.

Paul squinted at it, but all he said as he returned it was, "Wait for an update."

I didn't take that for a great deal of personal acceptance, but Bill went merrily on anyhow. "What I'm thinking is, she's too good to just run errands. So why not have her take over for me as desk assistant—I mean, now that I'm moving into being producer around here."

Paul raised one of his heavy eyebrows. "You think you've got that producer's job sewed up, do you?"

Bill cocked his head and grinned. "Yeah, I think so. Now Caroline here, she could get info on the phone. So if she can come in every morning at six instead of eight, I'll have her hit all the police and fire departments in the other towns around here and find out what we missed out on while we were closed up for the night."

Paul looked at me. "Think you can handle the milk run?"

"Sure!" I was trying hard to sound enthusiastic, though the truth is I have always absolutely detested having to get up early in the morning—especially during school vacation. "The kid," I grinned, "can handle anything."

"Okay," said Paul, giving me a little grin back. "Check in with the hospitals, too. The rest of the day—every fifteen minutes—you toddle over to the AP and UPI wire machines to see what's going on. Any story that even looks like we can use it, rip it off the roller and give it to Bill . . . or Douglas Johnson, the morning anchor. The other stuff you throw away. But not the *wrong* stuff. Think you can do that? Got that kind of judgment?"

"Yes, of course." At least I *thought* I had that kind of judgment.

"Oh. Then you already know how to pick out a news item that takes place somewhere else in the world but has a direct impact on our viewers here?"

"Well . . . I . . . I'll talk to Bill about it."

"Bill won't always be here when you're here. And you're going to have to pick it up some way."

"She will," Bill put in. "I'll give her some old broadcast scripts to study. And she'll keep her eyes open, right Caroline?"

"Yes!"

"Okay." Paul gazed at his watch. "Also every day, just about this time—and later at two o'clock—I want you to call the courthouses. Get the numbers from Bill. Find out if there are any interesting sentences and arraignments."

Before I could say "Fine," he turned away to answer the phone.

"You've been very nice to me," I told Bill as we stepped away from the assignment desk. "And I want to thank you."

"No sweat. I was in the same place you are a couple of years ago. But do you really know what an arraignment is?"

"No," I murmured, "but I was going to look it up."

"When Willy Brown was arrested for killing Mrs. Sorell, he was taken before a judge and charged with the crime and asked whether he pleaded guilty or innocent. That's an arraignment."

Paul Morris seemed to have the capacity to do a lot of things at the same time. He'd been arguing with someone on the phone and listening to us as well. "Speaking of Brown," he called out, "why don't you pull whatever old footage we've shot on him and take a look at it. Maybe Dave will come around on this story if I can make another pitch."

Bill showed me how to use the computer in the file room to locate the video cassette we needed. We brought it back to an open booth in the newsroom with a playback setup—and he let me run the equipment. Whirling past some other big story, we came to Barbara giving a lead-in from the anchor desk during the 11:00 P.M. news.

"There has been a brutal murder in Ridgewood Park. Agnes Sorell, thirty-five-year-old wife of county treasurer Ben Sorell, was found this evening brutally beaten to death in the kitchen of her home."

The scene now shifted from Barbara at the desk to a patrol car pulling up to a sidewalk in front of a police station. It stopped, and a handcuffed black man of about fifty was dragged out of it. As he came closer to

where the camera must have been, he looked up at it
with shining eyes that were wide open and bewildered.

"Police," Barbara's voice went on while we watched,
"have taken into custody a migrant worker who was
employed on the Sorells' two-hundred-acre farm in nearby
Ridgewood Plains."

"Freeze it, right there," Bill said.

I stopped the machine—and had a weird sensation, as
if that man with his lost and helpless expression had
himself stopped to gaze at me.

"See anything?"

"Like what?" I asked.

"Take a look at his shirt."

It was brown, slightly torn, and hanging half in, half
out of his beltless pants. I looked closer and saw a long
thin reddish splotch running down the front, near his
heart. The stain, you mean?"

"It's dried blood."

Bill had said it calmly, but I shivered. He told me to
go on.

"We spoke," Barbara narrated, "to Captain DeLeon
of the Ridgewood Park police . . ."

Now the captain came on in his office saying, "Officers Sullivan and Munzie were on routine patrol in the
River Road area at approximately 7:30 P.M. They ob-
served a man, obviously dazed, walking along the side
of the road. When they approached to speak to him, he
turned and ran down the river embankment. The officers left their vehicle and gave chase. . . ."

The camera then went to Willy Brown being finger-
printed in the station, but the captain's voice stayed on.
"The suspect was then apprehended."

The tape went off, and once more Barbara was back

live in the studio. "The murder took place in this house located in the suburban community's most exclusive section."

Over her right shoulder appeared a smaller picture—a beautiful two-story house, perched above the river and surrounded by huge trees and perfect lawn.

Now the camera passed into the farm and swerved to show a cluster of low-lying shacks.

"Here," Barbara's voice went on as we began to see the place, "farm workers and their families who come up from the South in the late spring and early summer, live in clapboard dwellings like these. There is no running water here and no electricity."

There was a very short interview with a black family that lived in one of the shacks. It was just long enough for an old lady to say that Willy Brown was a quiet, religious person who didn't drink or quarrel. She and her husband—who sat quietly by as she spoke—couldn't believe he had hurt anyone.

"The blood on that man's shirt," I asked, "I guess it matched Mrs. Sorell's?"

"That's what they say. We've got that on the next cassette. But this is what I was looking for."

"So you think he's guilty."

"Guilty or not," Bill sighed, "I think he's dead in the water. The trial is a formality."

"Is Barbara going to be covering it?"

"Probably, since she started with Brown. Why?"

"Because I'd love to get a chance to go out with her!"

Up until then, I hadn't realized that Paul had left his desk to stand behind us and watch what was being shown. "Hey, kid," he said. "I've got some sad news for you. Interns and desk assistants here are *inside* people. They don't go out on stories."

My spirits went right down into my shoes. But then I felt Bill's hands pressing lightly on my shoulder with a silent take-it-easy message. "Weren't you supposed to be making the courthouse calls by now? Willy Brown isn't the only case there is."

I walked off slightly fuming and started making calls. And I was still at them when Barbara came back, looking pretty irritable herself.

But nothing fazed Paul, who, the second she entered, rapped out, "We got a rule about calling in when you finish an assignment. How come you didn't do it?"

"I tried. The two-way wasn't working. We've got great equipment in that mobile unit all right."

"They still got telephone booths out that way?"

"I wanted to get the videotape back here as soon as possible. Though I really don't know why."

"No explosion?"

"No explosion, right." She kept walking toward her office.

"That's why you're in such a mood?" he called after her.

"Don't be a jerk. I'm not in any kind of mood. —Hello, Caroline. Everything okay?" But before I could answer, she slammed the door behind her.

Listening to her typewriter clicking away behind her closed door, I made up my mind to tell Barbara that I understood what she was going through. As soon as the typing stopped, I stood up and went inside.

"We usually knock," she said, looking at me without any friendliness in her face.

I had the warning thought that I should back out

quickly, but I didn't. "Sorry. I won't take a minute. I
. . . uh . . . only wanted to thank you so much for
recommending me for this job and all."

"No problem." She turned back to the script she was
looking over.

"And I feel very strongly," I suddenly said, "that it
is really horrible of them to keep you locked into your
contract like this."

She turned in her seat and cocked her head to look at
me. "What are you talking about?"

"I . . . I mean," I started, "the quarrel you're having with them here."

"There isn't any quarrel," she said evenly.

"Well . . . uh . . . the difficulty."

"There isn't any difficulty."

"You . . . you told me about the legal problem." I
was stumbling all over myself.

"There aren't any problems." She stood up. "Did
you have a message for me?"

"N . . . no."

"Well, I'm sure you must be very busy, Caroline."

"Yes . . . I am."

"I'm not going to have very much time to be helpful
to you, I'm afraid. Excuse me, I have to go to the
editing room. Good luck." She passed by me and was
out of the room before I could say thank you.

Slowly I followed her out. Hurt and confused, I
spent the rest of the day feeling depressed. Somehow I
knew that my attempt at being Barbara's friend had set
things back a long, long ways.

Chapter 7

GETTING TO WORK at six o'clock in the morning was some job in itself. Once, my mother had to climb out of bed right after she got into it, to drive me. And on Friday, I actually dragged myself out of the house in pitch blackness, dusted off the rear reflector, and biked the whole five miles.

Fortunately I didn't have to bike home. When I was through for the day, Don unscrewed the bike's front wheel, shoved the whole bike into his little Toyota van, and drove me back home. Naturally, we got to talking about Barbara, and I told him what had happened between us.

"Ah, it had nothing to do with you," he said. "I've even heard her talking to Paul about you. She's really in your corner."

"Really? What did she say?"

"Well, that was between them. Private."

"Oh, please!"

"She said that he should try to give you all the experience you can absorb, and stop thinking about how short a time you were going to be there. That time isn't as important as a person's enthusiasm—and she didn't want to see you lose yours." Don broke into a little grin. "Though she said she didn't think anybody could beat it out of you with a stick."

"But then what I still don't understand is—why doesn't she talk to me?"

For a moment I thought I saw a trace of sadness crossing Don's face. "Barbara is different from most people," he said. "She doesn't like to be comforted when she's sick or hurting. She goes off alone," he added with a sigh, "and won't let anyone come near her until she's herself again and ready to come out." Then he pointed a finger at me. "But don't get me wrong. She'll do everything in the world for someone else."

When we got to the house, my mother was sitting out front on a lawn chair, soaking in the late afternoon sunlight. She was still in her nurse's uniform, but her hair was down over her shoulders, her eyes closed in a doze, and her face damp. Instead of helping me get the bike out of the car, Don picked up an ordinary camera and started to shoot still pictures of her.

"Hi there," he said, when her eyes fluttered open.

My mother sat up quickly. "What are you doing?"

"When I see character in a face," he said simply, while continuing to shoot, "I don't let it get by me."

"Mom, this is Don LeFever from the station. He drove me home."

"Make him stop," she cried, jumping to her feet. "Look at me!"

"That's what I'm doing. But don't worry—it's a present for your husband."

"I don't have a husband."

"I was hoping you'd say that. Are you going to accept my invitation?"

"To what?"

"Dinner."

By now she had marched testily to the porch steps, but suddenly she stopped and turned to face him. "Are you this fast with everyone?"

I was amazed; she was actually, well, practically, considering his offer.

"I only want to buy you a meal."

"Well, what about my daughter?" Mom asked.

He broke into a smile, which unfortunately made his rugged face just a little less handsome. His teeth weren't perfectly even—and there was a little space between the two in the top front. "They don't pay me that much."

"We can go somewhere cheap," my mom said.

"I believe in quality," he brightly shot back—making me think how absolutely charming he was in spite of not being as gorgeous as Daddy.

"Listen, everybody," I put in. "I'll be glad to make something for myself. And, to tell you the truth, I've O.D.'d on junk food and I really don't have much of an appetite."

My mother fixed him with a look. "I am going to talk to my daughter about you. If she gives me a good report, then I'll accept for another time."

"I'm a man of impulse," he said, turning my bike upside down to put the wheel back on.

"Well, I'm afraid you'll also have to be one of persistence." She started up the steps.

"I can be that, too, Caroline's mother."

"My name is Ida." And she pushed through the door.

Without another word, Don finished assembling my bike with a wrench he'd pulled from the van, gave a little farewell salute to the porch window, and left.

The second week of my internship was a repeat of the first one, except I was getting better at what I did. My work day was supposed to be over at 2:00 P.M., but most of the time I hung around to see the six o'clock broadcast being put together—volunteering for this or that—and hoping that Barbara would notice me.

Privately, she may have spoken up for me—but speaking *to* me was something else again. On Monday, I only caught a couple of glimpses of her. On Tuesday, I stationed myself outside the studio where she couldn't miss seeing me on her way to do the show—making sure it would look as if I was running an errand. This time Barbara showed that she recognized me by sort of nodding her head at me. It was a big nothing.

The job would have been, too, if I hadn't gotten after all the technical people to show me how everything worked. That was really interesting. Or at least it was learning stuff I thought I should know. But none of it was getting rid of the sinking feeling that my month on this internship was running out very fast—and everything that I really wanted to happen, *wasn't*.

Anyway, that's what I was down in the dumps about when, after the broadcast, I went back downstairs to get my sweater and leave. As I entered the newsroom, I

saw Barbara standing on the far side. I decided I wasn't
going to say anything. I just turned away and headed
for the closet.

"Don't you ever go home, Caroline?"

"Uh . . . no," I answered, only half turning to look
at her. "I've got two and a half weeks left, and I want
to learn whatever I can. . . ."

"Won't do you much good, will it, if you just hang
around here and don't fight for yourself."

"But—" I cried in exasperation, "I don't know
exactly how. There are all these *rules*!"

She broke into another grin. "Why don't you say,
'Barbara, can I go with you on Monday to see you
cover the verdict on the Willy Brown case?' "

"You mean it?" I was very excited. "But Paul
says—"

"Not to worry." She raised her voice so it would
carry across the newsroom. "Right now they're all
terrified of me here. And I'm keeping it that way."

And from the other side of the assignment editor's
counter, I could hear Paul Morris snort.

There were five days to get through in between, and I
hoped I would make it to Monday morning. I was also
looking forward to Saturday night. Not because I had a
date, but because my mother had one with Don.

I hung out in her bedroom as she got ready, and I
could tell she was excited, although she wouldn't admit
it. We reversed roles and I gave her the pre-date lecture
as she mumbled yesses back to me with nods of her
head without really listening.

I didn't see any radiant smiles or hear any songs of
joy floating over the bathwater. And let's admit, too,

that she was just a little skeptical about anything really happening between her and Don. In fact, she was the same old steady-as-a rock Ida Burns. But all that was only on the surface. I could feel the nervousness as they went off to dinner—and whatever—with my blessings. Afterwards, which was about one in the morning, I couldn't get a word out of her except that it was "nice" and he was "nice" and "Caroline, don't go making a big thing out of it. We'll see."

I was sleepless Sunday night, but Monday came at last, thank God, like it always does. I dressed extra nice and treated myself to a call-in cab ride out of my birthday savings.

The anchorman for the early morning news broadcast was there ahead of me, studying suggestions for stories Paul had left him from the night before, and looking over the wire bulletins. I set down the cup of hot chocolate I'd pulled out of one of the coin machines, then began to make my calls to the different police departments.

After a couple of hours, Paul and Bill arrived, followed a little later by reporters and photographers. They got their assignments and went out while I, meanwhile, did the same things I always did. The hours dragged on—and the truth is I didn't even see Barbara.

At lunchtime, I pulled an apple and a banana out of my lunch bag and hung around my desk until I caught sight of Don, who gave me a friendly wave. Naturally, I jumped up and trailed him, wanting to find out what was going on not only with Barbara, but with my mother as well, but he disappeared into the men's room.

Paul announced that there was something that had been returned by mistake to the post office. I should hurry right over to pick it up. That was the last thing I wanted to be stuck with. Suppose Barbara came and went without me?

I wasn't going to put that into words, but I didn't have to. "Relax, Caroline. Even if they come in with a verdict, it won't be announced until they convene the court again at two o'clock. You'll go over before that."

I flew out of the building, picked up the package I was sent for, and flew back. When I arrived, Barbara and Don were just leaving by the side door for the parking lot. Another few seconds and they would have gone off without me!

I hurried over. "What's happening? I thought we weren't leaving for a while yet."

"Stop talking," Barbara snapped. "If you're coming, come."

I had already made one mistake with Barbara, and I didn't want to make another. "Are you . . . sure it's okay, I mean?"

"I asked you, didn't I?"

"Ten seconds!" I cried, and blasted into the newsroom.

I probably made it in less than five, but the station-wagon was already backing out of its spot when I raced back again. Don stopped for me, but Barbara looked annoyed at the interruption. I sank into the seat behind her, wondering what had happened. There was no way of finding out—we drove across town in absolute silence.

"Let me out," she impatiently told Don, while he was still moving through the traffic in front of the courthouse. He brought the car to a stop just long enough for her to hop out and head for the building.

I was going to follow her, but he stopped me. "Leave her alone. There's no rush."

"Then what's going on?"

Without answering, he drove farther on until we turned into a parking lot that circled around behind the courthouse.

"Is it something I've done?"

"No, it's—Barbara just heard that the job the network offered her went to somebody else."

"But I thought she couldn't take it anyway."

"Still," he said, getting out, "nobody likes to hear that kind of news." He walked around to the passenger side and started to take out his camera, video cassette recorder, and a collapsible light.

"Let me carry something. That must all weigh a thousand pounds."

"Thanks, but I'm used to it."

We headed for the building together and began to climb a flight of stairs. "What should I do now, Don?"

"Hang in with me. Look, listen—and don't say anything."

"But I can't help having the feeling that she's angry with *me*."

"The woman who got the job at the network instead of Barbara," Don said as we swept through the entrance, "was someone she trained."

Then I suddenly realized what he was saying. "But I'm not any competition for her," I mumbled. "I'm only sixteen years old!"

"Nothing says it has anything to do with reason, luv. But this old world has a way of setting good people against each other."

We hurried down a hallway to one of the courtrooms.

"Top of the day, Michael O'Shea," Don sang out. "Anything exciting happened yet?"

"Nothing yet," the man in an attendant's uniform answered. "The jury's still out, and His Honor is eating."

"That I don't doubt, for the man's always feeding. But then, with this bunch, they are *all* out to lunch!" O'Shea laughed aloud and Don laughed with him. "But now, where's Channel 8? Are they coming?"

The attendant shook his head. "They've already gone upstairs. Trial, Part Two."

"Uh oh." Then Don lowered his voice. "But have they come up with any news?"

"That I don't know."

Don rested his free left hand on the man's arm. "But you'll tell me if they do?"

"Don, you know you can always count on it."

"And Mike, you know, I'll put an *amount* on it." He gave the attendant a meaningful wink, and moved on to the elevator. "Do you know what that's all about?" he asked me as he pushed the button.

"I think so."

"It's called developing your sources."

"But weren't you acting like a reporter?"

"I was a reporter once."

"Then why did you give it up?"

"I don't care for talking to people all that much."

I have to say that I liked Don. I was beginning to like him more and more. But I couldn't help thinking—with my mother in mind—that he was a strange man. Then again, some people would consider my mother strange, too.

Chapter 8

THERE WERE A lot of people milling around the lobby outside the second-floor courtroom—including a camerawoman who smiled a hello at Don, and her partner, a reporter I recognized from Channel 8. He was talking to Barbara as we joined the crowd.

I didn't want to even attempt making conversation with Barbara. I figured that wasn't in my best interest right now.

"So, what do we do now?" I asked Don.

"Nobody knows you around here. Why don't you slide on over to the lawyers—see what they're saying about the case."

I looked around at all the people crowding the narrow corridor. "How can I tell which ones they are?"

"Find the suits and ties. Briefbags, too. The rest are mostly spectators. . . . That's a likely group over there by the cooler."

I wandered up to the water fountain near where a group of people had gathered.

"I missed Giezel's summary to the jury. How was it?" one of them asked a man who had come up just behind me.

"Need you ask, Al?" a woman member of the group put in.

"That bad?"

"Pathetic," she said. "Almost nonexistent. I can't understand how any judge in his right mind could have appointed a lawyer as weak as Giezel is to represent a defendant on a Murder One. Maybe, just maybe, I'd let him handle a jaywalking case—or passing through a stop sign. And even that, I'm not sure of."

"He doesn't," said another lawyer, "develop any kind of plausible theory for the defense."

"What gets me," said still another, "is that he never put his man on the stand to testify."

"Brown may have a previous conviction—some violent crime—that would have come out if he did," the man named Al said. "The DA could have crucified him with that."

"Okay," the woman replied, "but you have to chance it if you don't have any other evidence to present. They had the shirt that matched up with Mrs. Sorell's blood and the man's fingerprints were inside the house. All Giezel tried to do was cross-examine the arresting cops—and that wasn't going to get him anywhere. At least not the way he went about it."

The man named Al chuckled. "I get the impression, Bernice, that you don't give high grades to the noble Giezel for the defense?"

"He didn't even move the court to have the defendant's handcuffs removed before the jury came in. That's a clear tip-off to them that everyone thinks he's a murderer.''

"Sounds like a fair description of that woman's killer to me.''

"You're a lawyer," she shot back, "and you've already got him convicted. See what I mean?''

"Look at the evidence.''

"That doesn't mean he shouldn't get a skilled defense. In fact, it's all the more reason.''

Al turned to where I was drowning myself in an endless stream of water. "You finding this interesting?''

"Very much," I said. "And may I ask you a question?''

"I think we have to go inside," one of the lawyers said, backing away.

I looked around and saw O'Shea, the attendant, moving along in our direction, asking everyone to enter the courtroom and take their seats.

"You, too," he said, blocking my attempt to move against the crowd and get back to Don, whom I'd left in the hall. "We're bringing the defendant in now.''

"But I'm with Channel 12.''

"I know, but we have to clear a path to bring in the defendant.''

Walking backwards so I wouldn't miss anything, I saw the elevator open and several armed troopers step out of it with Willie Brown. His hands were cuffed behind his back and officers held him by each arm.

Even without all of that, there was something absolutely defeated about the man slowly shuffling along with his head cast down. It was so sad that I really wanted to look away. But then I reminded myself that I

was a newsperson and this was exactly the sort of thing
I had to get used to and even learn how to describe. I
stopped inside the courtroom close to the doorway and
waited to have the best look at him that I could get. He
seemed, I thought, so terribly alone. . . .

"Will everyone please be seated!" the attendant called.

While they marched Willy Brown down to the front
of the crowded courtroom, I found a seat for myself
near the back. After a two or three minute wait another
attendant called out: "All rise!" The judge swept in as
we stood up. I turned to see if I could locate Barbara
and spotted her standing in the back, just inside the
door. Through the little glass window, I could see Don
standing beyond her in the lobby with the minicam
perched on his shoulder.

Up to now there had been a certain amount of chit-
chat going on throughout the courtroom. But when the
twelve jurors filed in and took their seats in the special
box, everyone fell silent.

"Have you reached a verdict?" the jury foreman was
asked.

"Yes, we have, Your Honor."

"And what is your verdict?" the judge asked.

"Guilty as charged of murder in the first degree."

"Very well. Mr. Giezel, do you wish to poll the
jurors individually to test the verdict?"

"Er . . . yes . . ."

I didn't want to stay for any more. Quickly, I stood
up and walked out of the courtroom, not sure of what to
do next. By the time I got into the corridor, I saw that
Barbara was already preparing to attack her target. She
carefully took aim as, soon afterward, the crowd came
pouring out behind me.

"Mr. Giezel?"

The lawyer for Willy Brown, a stocky, middle-aged man with a fringe of white hair running around behind his ears, stopped in front of her. "Yes?"

Before she asked her next question, Barbara turned suddenly to me—the first evidence I had that she even knew I was there. "Go get the DA—and see if you can bring Mr. Sorell, too. They should be together."

She turned quickly back to the defense lawyer, giving me no chance to ask what Sorell looked like. I saw why. The other reporter was already descending on us.

"Why did you fail to put the defendant on the witness stand?" she asked as I started to look around for the DA among the passersby.

"It was for good and sufficient legal reason, Ms. Richie, believe me. I don't want to go further than that. Besides I didn't think the prosecution had a good case to prove guilt beyond a reasonable doubt. I still don't. But the jury disagreed with me."

I had already moved away, but his voice didn't sound upset by the verdict at all.

"Does that mean," the other reporter now shot in, "that you intend to file an appeal?"

I didn't get to hear the answer because I noticed one of the lawyers I had more or less met at the water cooler coming along in my direction. "Excuse me," I said, stopping him. "Can you point out the DA?"

He looked over his shoulder and pointed to a group of men standing near a wall talking together. "He's the one with the big smile on his face, getting all the congratulations."

I walked over and, not knowing how fast Barbara wanted him, broke right into the conversation. "Uh

. . . I'm sorry . . . but I'm with Channel 12. Ms. Richie would like to interview you.''

The annoyed look that began with my rudeness disappeared immediately. ''Always delighted to speak with Miss Richie,'' he replied, beaming at me. ''Lead on.''

''Would you know where Mr. Sorell is?''

''I'm Ben Sorell,'' said a short, broad-shouldered man who had been quietly standing next to him. Unlike the DA, he was very serious-looking, and his voice so soft that I hardly heard him. ''I'm sorry,'' he told me, ''but I'm feeling very tired and I think I'm going to decline.''

The DA gave him a look.

''All right, I'll say something.''

We started to go, but before I could lead them to her, Barbara came to us.

There were no hellos. She jumped right in. ''Your adversary claims that you took unfair advantage by trying to prejudice the jury in this case. Do you have any comment on that?''

''Pure nonsense.''

''He meant by the way in which you spoke of the defendant, calling him 'a true criminal who has no pity or human feelings.' ''

''I won't go over the details of the beating, Barbara. I think that Mrs. Sorell's husband, who is standing here, has already had to endure quite enough during the coroner's testimony. Again I say, the facts speak for themselves.''

Barbara extended the microphone to Mr. Sorell and, in as gentle a manner as possible, asked for his reaction to the verdict.

There was a long pause while Ben Sorell pondered his answer. The conversation around us subsided, and everyone waited. "I had thought," he began slowly, "that I might take some satisfaction in vengeance. But that, I realize, won't bring this wonderful, vibrant woman back." He paused again, as if gathering strength. "All I can say is, I feel that justice has been done. And I think that the district attorney deserves my thanks—and the public's—for an excellent job."

"Clear the hall, please," a voice rang out. "They're bringing the defendant to the elevator."

The remaining lawyers and spectators were already heading for the stairs by the time two armed guards came out of the courtroom, moving ahead side by side to sweep the place clear.

We waited, along with the other television crew and a few newspaper reporters, for Willy Brown to be led out. As soon as he emerged, everyone rushed for him at once.

"What do you have to say about your conviction?" Barbara's rival got in first.

Brown, who was not allowed to stop, gazed back with eyes that at first did not seem to understand.

"Is there anything you want to tell everyone?" Barbara asked, walking backward, as we retreated with him to the elevator. "Anything you want to tell us at all."

Willy Brown seemed at last to come out of his thoughts. "There is nothing," he answered softly, "that I *can* say to you. And there is nothing that I have to say to my Maker. The Lord already knows . . . and I'll wait now for His justice." He fell silent and stepped with the troopers into the elevator.

Something stayed with me as he disappeared behind the closing door—a feeling that there was more to do, more to know. It just seemed wrong that everything should be breaking up like this—that it was all over and the reporters were going away.

"Barbara," I suddenly blurted.

"Yeah?"

"I . . . uh . . . was listening to the lawyers who were watching the trial. They all felt that the only possible reason for Mr. Giezel to stop Brown from testifying for himself would be to keep the jury from learning about any violent crime he might have committed before. But one of them said that she didn't think that was enough—"

Barbara cut me off. "You have something in mind? What is it?"

"Well, only . . . I just thought that—" My voice broke, and I had to stop and collect my thoughts. "Well, there's something about the way Brown is acting—as if this was all he could expect whether he was guilty or not. I sort of think it would really be interesting to kind of get him to talk about how he feels . . . and how he sees everything."

"That's a really fine idea." Barbara interrupted coldly. "Why don't you do it?"

"I didn't mean—"

"I don't care what you didn't mean," she snapped. "This is a wrap!" She turned on her heels and strode away from me.

"Don," I gasped. "What did I do?"

"My fault, not yours, Caroline. I'm sorry. I should have asked you to just watch."

"She really thinks that I could—or would—compete with her? That's—that's unbelievable."

"No, she doesn't think that."

"Then *why*?"

"I can't explain her to you now, kid. I have to go edit this. Look, it's late for you anyway, so maybe you ought to get home from here. Talk to you tomorrow," he said, starting to back away from me. "And don't take it so personally. She yelled at me, too. And give a big hello from me to your mother."

I nodded, and watched him go. The growing emptiness of the building made me feel even more depressed. As I left the courthouse, I began telling myself that my whole internship at Channel 12 might just as well have ended right there. So long as there was no chance left of working with Barbara Richie, it was all over.

I was just about to cross the street when a patrol car passed in front of me. It was a sudden reminder that my problems hardly compared to Willy Brown's. If *I* felt cut off from everything right now, what must that man be feeling?

I stopped at the curb and thought about the fact that I was still a journalist—if only on a school paper. There was a Woolworth's store down the block, and I ran into it. Three minutes later, I ran out again with a notebook and pen. I raced up the courthouse steps and got to the entrance door just as the attendant was about to lock it from the inside.

"Mr. O'Shea," I blurted. "Where did they take Willy Brown?"

He didn't remember me at first.

"Channel 12," I said to remind him.

"Ah, yes. He's down in the holding pen, I suppose. They wouldn't have transferred him yet."

"Where do I find it?"

Chapter 9

HE GAVE ME directions, which led to a basement. I walked around there until I came across two armed troopers sitting on stools before a metal door.

One of them stood up and blocked my way. "Where are you going?"

"I want to interview Willy Brown."

"Interview?" he snorted. "You kidding? Let's see your press pass."

"She's okay," said the other officer. "I saw her with the DA upstairs." He turned to me. "Channel 12, right? You're working with Richie."

"Yes," I said quickly. "Mr. O'Shea told me I'd find Brown down here."

The first officer unlocked the metal door, then made sure to step in ahead of me. I walked into a windowless little room at the other end of which was a wall of bars. Behind it was Willy Brown.

For a moment I had visions of the guard opening the cell and letting me in with the man, the way they sometimes do in the movies. I have to say that whatever sympathy I'd had for Willy Brown when either he or I were somewhere else vanished in a hot flash.

"Sit over here please," the officer said, motioning me to an out of reach place against the doorway wall. "Brown, you stay where you are. This lady from the TV news wants to talk to you."

Now that I was perfectly safe, my courage came back. "Uh, officer, can I talk to him alone?"

"Sorry. At the prison maybe, but not here." He folded his arms and leaned back against another wall.

"Uh, Mr. Brown? I'd like to talk to you, if you don't mind."

He studied me quietly. In fact, everything about him was quiet, calm. As he sat there, waiting, I grew more and more uncomfortable. All at once I asked myself, what am I doing here? I've got to be crazy to want to interview a convicted criminal.

"Mr. Brown," I began shakily. "I want you to know that . . . that I really can't help you in any way. I mean, with your case. I'm just doing this for my sch—" I remembered the guard standing there. "I mean, it's just research."

Willy Brown nodded slowly.

"Could you—" I broke off and began again. "Uh . . . you made a statement before about leaving justice to God. Are you saying that the jury's verdict was unjust?"

"Doesn't matter what I say," he replied softly, with a half-smile forming on his lips. "You just told me that. And I truly think you're right."

"Well, but—no one really knows your side of it. Don't you think people would like to hear it?" I opened my pad.

"Tell me, do you think I'm going to get the death penalty?" he suddenly asked.

I choked up. "I . . . really don't know."

"My lawyer says I've got a fifty-fifty chance at a life sentence, but I don't know if I want that. I spent a year in jail once, and I don't want to go through that again." He stood up from his bench and gripped the bars of the detention cell. "This is enough of a reminder. . . ."

"Is that why you didn't go on the stand to testify? Because you've been convicted of something before?"

"Yes, my lawyer said it would hurt the case for the jury to know." He shrugged and smiled. "But it didn't seem to matter much, did it?"

"Well, what had you done?"

"Oh, I stole a crate of oranges down in Gainesville, Florida."

"A crate of oranges? That was *it*?"

"It was enough, I guess."

"When was this, Mr. Brown?"

"I'd just turned sixteen."

"What!"

"Well, I was big for my age. They told me later I could have had what they call 'youthful offender' treatment and stayed out of prison because of my age and having no record. But no one," he said with a little smile, "told me then."

"Why did you take the oranges?"

"Well, I was hungry. It was hard times then and I couldn't find a job. And there was an old man with me, too—I'd sort of adopted him as my uncle. He couldn't run as fast as I could." Mr. Brown broke into a chuckle. "Nobody could in those days. But it slowed me down a bit—and they caught me."

"Were you arrested any other times?"

"Never even stopped for a speeding ticket. I had my own grocery store for twenty-five years until my wife died. Then I just . . . well it was hard for me, all those memories. My sister took my daughter, and I just began to wander. And working in the fields, you know, gives a man time to think about what's important and what isn't . . . ." Willy Brown fell silent again.

"But it doesn't make any sense to me!" I said. "I don't see why your lawyer would tell you not to testify just because you stole some oranges when you were only a kid."

"Well, I thought the same way, too. But I had to take his advice. He was the man they gave me—and I couldn't afford anyone else."

"Do you think Mr. Giezel did a good job?"

He gave a little laugh. "Let's just say I got what I paid for."

I looked up from my pad. "Forgive me, Mr. Brown, but you talk as if you don't *care* whether you had a good defense or not. I don't understand that."

He took another long look at me. "You're a young person—and you may not know about how some things go in this world. And maybe you'd better think about all the questions you're asking. You sure you want to find out?"

For a moment I felt scared, although I didn't know why. "Yes, I do. . . . And I'd appreciate it if you'd tell me about the day of the . . . the . . ."

"Murder," he said, with a look that went straight

into my heart. Then he paused, and, with relief, I dropped my gaze to the notepad.

"I have two sisters," he began. "And my oldest one is down in Virginia. I got a letter a few days before saying that she was very sick in the hospital, maybe dying. I wanted to go down to see her, but I'd already sent my last pay for the care of my daughter. So I needed to get an advance on my job, but the manager wouldn't do that because he didn't know if I'd come back. Anyway, a friend of mine—someone I *thought* was my friend—knew the manager's boss, Mr. Sorell. He'd worked for him on the farm two or three years before, but I had never met the man. So we agreed to go together to see him—and George could put in a word for how dependable I was—and that George would make it good if I didn't come back."

"What was George's last name?"

"Blackwell. He came over to my shack that night, but his car wasn't working right. So we walked from the farm to that road where the Sorells live. . . . About two, three miles, I guess. It was a nice, warm night, and we were taking our time. But when we got close to the house, George stopped me. There was a woman screaming. Terrible screams. They were coming from the house. One right after another. You could tell someone was being beaten in there . . . bad."

I heard a little sigh behind me and turned my head. The officer standing guard caught my eye as he lit a cigarette.

"We didn't know what to do," Brown went on. "George grabbed my arm and said, 'Come on man, let's get away from here! This isn't our business.' But I *couldn't* leave because I . . . well, I just couldn't. I had to do *something*—and I ran up to the house by myself. The door wasn't locked, so I went in and started running through the rooms—and I found her in the kitchen. Lord, her face was all beat up and there was blood all over it. She was gasping as if she was choking on her own blood and hanging on to the end of the table. But then she started to fall while I was running up to her, and—''

Nearby, the officer gave a little cough.

''And I caught her!'' Brown insisted, as if the policeman were calling him a liar.

''That was when I heard a door slam and then a car go flying off. Mrs. Sorell slipped out of my arms to the floor and I could tell that she was dead. . . .'' Willy Brown's voice slowed down. ''I'd seen death before. I could tell it. . . . And then I got worried about myself. I thought that if the police came, they would say that I did it. That I came to rob her or worse. . . .''

He stopped once more to gaze at the cop, who was slowly shaking his head. For all of Willy Brown's talk about his leaving the truth for his Maker to decide, I could tell that he *wanted* to be believed.

''Go on, Mr. Brown, please.''

''I ran out of the house as fast as I could. I didn't see George anywhere, and I was too upset at first to even remember which direction we had come from. I started running the wrong way down the road. Then I stopped myself and saw all the blood that was on me. I was just about to leave the road and rush down to the river to wash it all off when the police car came towards me and I . . . I went into a panic!''

''Did you tell this to anyone?''

"Yes—the police, the man from the district attorney's office—and my lawyer, Mr. Giezel."

"Did anyone look for George Blackwell so he could back up your story?"

"My lawyer says he did, but he couldn't find him. I told him that maybe Mrs. Uggams and her husband could find George, but I don't know if he went to them. . . . I don't think he really believed much in my case." Brown fell into a deep silence.

"Who are the Uggams?" I asked softly, just to start the conversation again. "Mr. Brown?"

". . . A dear couple . . . migrants like myself . . . They work on the same farm with me. I would have loved to see them, but the police wouldn't let anyone visit before the trial but my lawyer."

"You must be feeling very much alone."

"No." He sighed. "I have my Savior. Only I have to keep reminding myself of that."

"Do you . . . do you have any idea who might have killed her?"

"Yes," he said slowly, looking up to carefully grip me with his eyes. "I've known all along who did that. Her husband."

Brown's words chilled me like an icicle pressed against my back. "Mr. *Sorell*?"

"That's right. She said, 'My husband Ben beat me.' She said it just when I caught her, before she fell to the ground."

"Miss, are you finished?" the guard asked in a tired voice.

"Just a minute. Mr. Brown, you must have told your *lawyer* what she said to you?"

"Many times. I told the police and I told him. But he

said that if I repeated that in court, I'd only make everything worse for myself. Because there was no proof, and Mr. Sorell is a very important man.''

''What did the police say?''

'' 'You got her blood all over you!' ''

The guard ground out his cigarette. ''You all set with your interview?''

''Yes, I think so. Mr. Brown, I have to go now. I'm very sorry all this has happened to you. Thank you for talking to me.''

Willy Brown nodded, then sank back into that deep, calm silence as I passed through the door.

''You didn't believe him, did you?'' I asked the guard when we closed it behind us.

''Let me put it this way. I used to work at Greeway prison. Practically every inmate has a story how he was framed—and most of them sound a lot better than this one. I think they even get to believe those stories themselves.''

''But it could be true?''

''Maybe, but what can you do?''

''Well, thank you for letting me in.''

The farther I walked away from that holding cell and the courthouse, the more I realized that I didn't have to think that there was nothing I could do.

Not yet.

Chapter 10

A HALF HOUR LATER I plowed back into the newsroom, looking for Barbara. I didn't want anyone to stop me no matter what was going to happen. All the way over, my only thought had been to risk having her blow up at me again by going straight to her with what I'd learned. It was just because I dreaded what she'd do that I had to get this over with. Maybe she'd forget about my reminding her of someone else and see how important my information was. And that I was bringing it to *her*!

I looked around, but didn't see her. The place was crowded with reporter-photographer teams rushing to get their news packages ready for the broadcast. Paul was busy on the two-way, trying to get someone to report in. The sportscaster was reading the wires for something he could could use. And Bill sat at his typewriter, pounding out copy for the anchorpeople to recite.

Then suddenly, Barbara stormed into the newsroom calling, "The footage we shot is terrible! Where's Don? He's got black streaks all over my face."

"Relax," Bill called from his desk. "There was a glitch in the tape, but—"

"Relax? I look terrible!"

"I'm sure Don can edit it out."

"Yeah? Well, I want to hear *him* tell me."

All this shouting should have stopped me, but I knew that if I didn't speak up right then, it would only get harder. "Barbara," I said hoarsely, stepping in front of her. "I know I'm being persistent and this is the wrong time to talk to you. But can I do it anyway? This is important."

"I can't *talk* to you now, Caroline."

"Hey, Caroline!" Paul was waving me over. "You better leave her alone," he said in a low voice as I went over to the counter.

"But I've got something to tell her about the Brown case."

"Tell me." He looked at his watch. "You've got thirty seconds. Shoot."

"But it'll take me longer!"

"Wasting time: twenty-five seconds."

I blurted out my story as best I could. But it was a mess. He kept looking at the second hand on his watch, which made me nervous. I had gotten in to see Willy Brown in the courthouse holding pen. Mrs. Sorell, according to what the defendant told me, had accused *her own husband* of the beating. And Brown had heard a car—probably his—drive off. There was a witness named George Blackwell who could back up his real reason for being there. That man had also heard the screaming before he ran away. Brown had told everything to his lawyer and also to the police, but no one had really looked into his story.

"Time's up."

"I just want to say that all the lawyers who were watching the trial couldn't get over the fact that the judge had appointed such a rotten lawyer as Mr. Giezel to defend someone in a murder case."

"Finished?"

"Yes."

"Did you ask Brown why—if Blackwell was his good buddy—he never came forward on his own at the trial?"

"No, but I think . . ."

Paul stared up at me. "What you *think* is that you are definitely a reporter now. "No," he corrected himself, "an investigative reporter. Right?"

I didn't answer. As far as I was concerned I had done a good job, and I wasn't going to back down.

"Look what we got here, Bill. Stonewall Burns."

Bill had been standing nearby, listening—and I had thought that he was interested in what I'd come up with. But now he was frowning, too. I couldn't take it anymore. "Somebody want to tell me what I did wrong?"

"You misrepresented yourself," Paul said, full of a kind of trembling anger, "as a representative of this station—which you are *not*. That's how you got in. That's how you got the interview. And this is strictly unethical. And what's more, I resent it."

"I'm . . . I'm sorry. I really am, Paul." I fell silent while he pondered, I think, whether to fire me.

". . . Okay," he said at last. "Let's forget it."

Bill leaned over the assignment desk. "Still sounds like a story though. With a little luck I think it could be a winner . . . a real biggie."

Paul dumped a wet cigarette in a tray, and reached for another. "Yeah, if there's something to it. Ten to one it's only jailbird. talk."

"Worth finding out though."

"Could be—if we were in a big market like Philadelphia or New York—where we'd have the budget for an investigating team. But there's barely enough reporters on deck to cover the daily hard news."

"Why can't I look on my own?" I asked.

"Still the investigator, huh?"

Bill broke into a big smile. "She's done pretty well up to now."

"It won't interfere with the other things I do," I said. "Just in my spare time, after work."

Paul studied me. "You have some idea how to go about it?"

"Isn't the next thing to look for George Blackwell?"

"You got it."

"The assignment?" I beamed.

He pointed a finger at me. "No, you get no assignment from me. I want to make this clear. What you do on the outside, that's on your own. Which means, you can't get in places by saying you're from our newsroom. And you can't use our photographers or video equipment. Now if you still want to look into it, that's up to you." He thought for a moment, then added, "But if you come up with something—and as soon as you do—bring it to me. Then we'll see."

"Yes, sir!"

Looking back on it, I don't know what I was so happy about; Paul hadn't really given me much, but it was still enough to keep me going.

Chapter 11

My MOM WAS on duty at the hospital, and I didn't want to go home to an empty house, when I had so much news to tell *someone*. I rushed over to Helen's place instead. And there I found her, in the backyard, mooning over her sinking love affair, the third this summer. The latest tragedy was with Moe Stern, a boy from her driver's ed class. I had learned by now that no matter what I said, it was best to let Helen go through these up-and-down romances. She wasn't very receptive to advice.

Helen did her best to pay attention to me. But all the while I was talking, she kept her eye on the telephone, which was stretched all the way out from the house, so she could pounce on it the moment it rang.

"I think it's really exciting," she said when I was through. "And I know you'd like me to drive you around to look for this man, but I really can't do it now.''

"It's not just for me, Helen. I think it's a lot better for you than just sitting around, waiting for Moe to call. It seems to me he isn't going to do it anyway.''

"He *will* call. I got hold of his mother and she promised me faithfully to get him to do it tonight.''

"Helen! Aren't you afraid he's going to resent you for involving his mother.''

"What difference does it make? He probably resents me now. I just want to hear from his own mouth that it's all over.''

"Please take my advice and come with me.''

"Why don't you see that I can't! I've got to stick by the phone.''

"Okay . . .''

"But . . . you could stay for supper and we can play Scrabble and maybe you'll even sleep over. That would be great. It's been such a long time—you've been so busy.''

"I know—and I'd love it, too. Only I've got to get going on this thing right away. It's a person's life.''

"Can't a person's life wait just one more day?''

I glared at her. "That's really something to say.''

She stared back. "Look at what *you* said! You make the whole thing sound so . . . soap opera dramatic.''

That ticked me off. "Helen! How would you like to have just been found guilty of murder?''

"I can't relate to it. I never murdered anybody.''

"Maybe he never did either!''

"Maybe—but I don't think anybody would ever arrest *me* for it.''

"Perhaps you're just lucky to be this safe,'' I said,

growing angry at the selfishness I thought she was showing. "Perhaps that's why all you do is just sit around here inventing terrible problems for yourself."

She jumped off the swing. "If you feel that way, I don't want you in my house."

"I'm not in your house."

"Then I don't want you in my backyard!"

"Now who's getting dramatic?"

"Well, that's how I feel about it."

I took a step backward. "You're absolutely sure?"

"Yes, I'm positive."

"Look," I said, giving her one last chance. "Do you want to talk about this?"

"No, I don't want to talk about it."

"Suits me." I turned on my heels and went back through the house to the front door. Even as I stepped outside, I was beginning to realize that I was wrong, too. Helen had been dreaming of falling in love for so long. And then suddenly there had been this Moe Stern. I turned around in order to say, okay—I'm sorry.

But, before I could get the words out, she slammed the door in my face.

I started to feel miserable. Helen and I both had our problems and we were taking them out on each other— which wasn't fair. I headed for the nearest pay phone, took a deep breath, and called my friend.

"This isn't *him*!" I barked as soon as she answered. "It's only me, okay? And I'm not going to tie up your phone. I just wanted to say that our friendship is too important—"

"Where did you go?" she broke in. "I ran out of the

house a moment later and you were gone! I'm sorry, Caroline. All is forgiven!''

"Okay," I said. "Let's forget about it."

"No, you're not going to forget about it while you're still feeling lousy. You'll just resent me later. So let me tell you something."

"What?" I asked in a small voice.

"You're my best and only friend in the whole world. I really think you're doing a wonderful and noble thing about this Willy Brown. I can't tell you how much I admire you for it. And for being part of what's going on. . . . But I can't go now; I need to hear from Moe. Maybe tomorrow after he calls I can help you. Just please don't go by yourself today, because it could be dangerous."

"Why do you think that?"

"Don't *you* think it could be?"

"Nobody said anything about it at the newsroom."

"So that means it's not dangerous?"

"I'll be careful."

"Ask your mother to go with you."

"She's on duty tonight."

There was a long silence. "Please, Caroline, don't go alone. You're right that a man's life is important, but so is yours. Wait one more day for me. I know Moe's going to call me tonight. Don't be in such a hurry."

"Helen, you don't understand. I've only got the rest of this week, then next week—and after that there won't *be* a Channel 12 for me anymore."

"Caroline, let's be honest about this. I said that you were doing a noble thing, but you are really out to prove something, aren't you?"

"Come on, I'm not out to prove anything."

"You know what I mean. You want to show everybody—and yourself—what you can do."

"Sure, that's part of it."

"How big a part?"

"Very big!"

"Fine," she said. "At least you're being honest."

"Can I go now?" I grumbled. "I thought you were expecting the love of your life to call."

"I'll worry about that. And you tell me first how you are going to get way out there?"

". . . On my bike."

"It'll take forever."

"Don't worry about me. And he is probably trying to get you right now. So good-bye."

"Wait a minute," she cried.

"No, I'm going." And I stormed off.

I had to go home first to get my bike and, just as I got there, I heard the phone ringing. I decided to ignore it because it was probably Helen, wanting to give me more of a hard time. Only maybe someone else can say no to ten straight rings while they're changing clothes. I can't. Finally, I snapped it up.

"Caroline, don't you dare go anywhere—and at night—without me!" It was my mother.

"That fink! She called you at the hospital! Mom, I know what I'm doing and I'll be fine."

"You certainly will. Because it's out."

"Please let me explain to you why I've got to go."

"No, I haven't got the time to listen now."

"But you have to!"

We argued back and forth for a while, until—as much to get rid of me and get back to work as for any other reason—she promised to drive me around herself the next afternoon.

"But that's your day off."

"What are days off for—except to get into trouble?"

Chapter 12

"MORNING," PAUL SAID when he arrived at the newsroom loaded down with a bunch of big city newspapers. "Get anything yet on the big scoop?"

"Working on it," I muttered, before burying myself in my chore of the moment. I didn't want to tell him that I had to wait for my mother to drive me around.

Bill came over a little later. "Listen, I have to go out of town tonight and I won't be back until the day after tomorrow. But if you wait until then, I'll go out with you to the shacks. Those migrant farmers are very wary of outsiders, but they might talk a little easier if they saw me." Then he added with a smile, "It'll still be your story."

I thanked Bill for his offer, but I said I didn't want to wait.

Then, promptly at two o'clock, my mom picked me up and we headed for the outskirts of town. My idea was to go to the Sorell farm and speak to Mrs. Uggams, Willy Brown's friend. Maybe she could lead us straight to Blackwell. We took a regular highway out to Ridgewood Park, the little suburb where Mr. Sorell lived, and then a small country road that led to the farm area a couple of miles farther on.

We ran into problems when that road divided into two smaller ones, and there weren't any signs telling where anything led to. We picked one and drove on it for a few miles, then turned around, went back to the fork, and set out on the other one. What we saw was an eternity of trees. Finally, in desperation, my mother pulled over and waved down the only automobile we had seen in all this time.

The driver, a man in his forties, pulled his car to a stop and gave us a friendly grin. "How lost are you?"

"We don't know," my mother answered. "Can you direct us to the Sorell farm?"

"Well, you happened to ask me an easy one. I'm Mr. Sorell's manager. Can I help you?"

I nudged my mother in the side. "We're looking for someone," she said, giving away as little as possible.

"You sure you two are going to the right place?"

"Don't you have some farm workers living there?" I asked quickly.

"Yeah, we got a few. Why?"

My mother simply replied, "There's somebody we want to see."

He was still friendly, but trying to figure us out. "You social workers, health inspectors, or what?"

"I gave my mother another nudge. "Visiting nurse service," she said with a smile.

The lines across his face cleared up. "Same difference. Who's sick?"

"Oh, we're just making some follow-up calls."

"Listen," he said, "I'm running late." And with that he got in his car and drove off without telling us where the Sorrell farm was.

As he disappeared down the road, my mother turned to me. "Do you think your idol Barbara Richie could do better than that?"

"No, you were great."

"Thank you very much." She started up the car. "And now we can go home."

"But we can't! I've got to find that witness."

"We can't even find the Sorell farm."

"He was coming from that direction. We saw only a couple of dirt roads leading off it when we were down that way before."

"Perhaps he's not coming from the farm but going to it."

"Can't we just try?"

"What do we do if he shows up while we're there, Caroline? Would you enjoy having to give him a different explanation?"

"No."

"Neither would I."

"But Mother—"

"All right. We'll go down that road up ahead and take a quick look—but that will have to be it."

A left turn took us onto little more than a trail that we would have had to back up to get out of. "Mom," I said as we drove along, "you don't have to feel that I look up to Barbara Richie more than I do to you. And—"

"Caroline, I am not jealous."

"Let me finish. And, in fact, the more I see of her, the more I respect *you*."

"I'm sorry I started this business of comparing one person against another. It's not good for anyone, so let's stop it."

"Yeah, I guess you're right. Barbara's human just like everyone else. And speaking about being only human, what's up with you and Don? You haven't seen him lately or talked about him either."

"Because I think he likes a certain anchorwoman a bit too much."

I turned to her in amazement. "You mean Barbara? He told you that?"

"More or less. I gathered it from the way he spoke of her."

"So you're not going to see him anymore?"

"Caroline, your mother has a few bumps of her own from out of the not-too-distant past."

"That's the place!" I suddenly yelled. "Those are the shacks I saw on the videotape. That's the farm."

Turning in through the gate up ahead, we pulled off to the right and came to a stop near a cluster of wooden buildings. A little girl with a ribbon in her hair studied us as we got out of the car. Three other children slowly joined her.

"Excuse me," I said. "Is there a grown-up here we can talk to?"

The oldest child vanished into the nearest shack and came out a moment later with an old woman.

"Yes?"

"Excuse me, but we're looking for Mrs. Uggams."

"I don't know anyone by that name," she rapped

out, giving a sharp wave to the children, then turned away from me and went back. They all followed her into the cabin, where several others were waiting just beyond the door.

I went up and peered inside. The place was fairly dark for such a bright afternoon. The floor was jammed with sleeping mats, some chairs around a wood table, a stove, and a very old refrigerator—but there was no sink. The woman lived here of course, but all these kids and the toys that lay strewn around gave me the idea that this was where the farm workers left their children for the day.

"Excuse me, are you sure Mrs. Uggams or her husband isn't around?" I asked again.

"I already told you," she snapped. "I'm busy."

"Caroline," my mother said, coming up behind me, "this lady may suspect we have come here on some kind of official business. She's probably afraid to talk to us."

"We're not with the government," I called to the woman. "We're friends of Willy Brown."

She gave me a sideways glance, then turned away again. "I'm very busy."

"Yes, but—where is Mrs. Uggams? It's very important that I speak with her—"

"She's not here. Her husband was fired."

"Fired?"

"Yes. The boss told them they weren't wanted here! Last I heard they got on a bus."

"To where?" But the woman only shrugged. "Do you know George Blackwell?"

"No!" She answered so quickly that I found it hard to believe her answer.

"Please, it's a matter of life or death."

"No!"

"Well, is there another person—"

"Caroline."

"Mother, I'm—"

"The manager is back."

I went quickly to the door. That same car was coming up along the road that led to the farm. "Mom, do you think he came to check on us?"

"I don't know, but let's get out of here."

"But I don't see what we have to be afraid of."

"I wish I *did* know. And I don't want to wait to find out. Hurry up."

I thanked the woman and jumped into the car. We managed to back up and turn around just as the manager's car swung in through the gate. For a moment we both held our breath. All he had to do was stop right there and block our way. Instead he drove straight into the field along another path rather than take the turn that led toward us.

There was no way of knowing whether he had missed seeing us or was simply ignoring us. We didn't wait to find out. We just drove.

"It may be a little late for me to sound like an intelligent mother, but I'm really sorry you've taken this on yourself," my mother said after we had put a little distance behind us.

"Mother, there's another farm road coming up. Let's try that."

"You really didn't hear me, did you?"

"Please! It's so important."

"So is our safety."

"That man didn't even bother us."

"But they fired Mr. and Mrs. Uggams. So they are doing *something*."

"Which is why we have to try some other places."

"*We* don't have to do anything."

"You mean I can go on my own?"

She brought the car to a stop. "Is that what you think I said?"

"No . . ."

"So you really think you can do this all on your own?"

"I'm not saying that."

"What *are* you saying?"

I didn't answer her. I suppose in a way I did think I could do this on my own.

Finally my mother broke the silence. "All right. I understand how much this means to you," she quietly said, and turned the car around. I gave her a big smile. My mom can come through when it counts.

There was a farm farther on up the other road. It had fewer shacks, and they seemed to be in better condition than at the Sorell farm. But we couldn't find anyone inside of them, so we started walking along the outside of the field to where two black men were working on a broken part of the fence.

I decided to get right to the point. "Hi," I said, "I'm trying to see if I can find out the truth about Willy Brown. Do you know who he is?"

"The truth is," said the younger of the two, "that he won't be around here for a long time, if you know what I mean."

"Well, I don't think he's guilty. Do you?"

The other man kept on working silently, but the younger one shrugged. "Jury says he did it, right?"

"Maybe there's a way to get a new trial. I'm looking for a man named George Blackwell. Do you know him?"

"Doesn't everybody?"

The older man straightened up and gave him a quick look to shut him up, then he turned to us. "My son here likes to act big and talk big. This George Blackwell, we don't know him."

I wasn't going to let it go at that, so I turned back to the boy. But he only looked away.

"Please believe me," I went on. "We are really trying to help."

"That's nice," said the older man, "but you see this hole in the ground?"

"Yes?"

"I can dig it all by myself. Don't need any help. See what I mean?"

"Well then, I guess I'll go ask some of the other people who work here."

"They don't know him either."

"Is it all right with you if I ask?"

"You do anything you want."

"Thank you anyway," I said, and we started walking farther into the field.

There was a group of people up ahead, but as we approached, they started to walk off. I looked back over my shoulder. The man we had just left was signaling them with his arms to stay away from us!

"So much for this," my mom said firmly. "We are going home."

Glumly, I agreed. I was feeling defeated and wasn't into talking very much as we started heading back. But then, just when we were pulling up to the highway entrance near Ridgewood Park, I had a thought. "Mom, let's go past the Sorell house."

"What for? Caroline, we are not going to find your missing witness at the murdered woman's home."

"Can we do it anyway?"

"Where do you get this obstinacy from?" she asked, making a turn in a brand-new direction.

"From you, I think."

We got on River Road and, as we drove around, my mother began to wonder how we would identify the place.

"I saw it on that tape in our files. It's Tudor style."

"Do you know what Tudor style is?"

"Well, not exactly, but it's sort of English. There's the house!"

"That's not English at all. It's Spanish."

"Well, that's it anyway."

My mother pulled the car over.

"These houses across the road from it, what are they doing here?" I was looking at two much smaller places that were separated from each other by a lawn.

"You've lost me."

"On the tape that was made after the arrest, the Sorells' house looked so fancy and surrounded by woods and everything, that I just didn't imagine there'd be other places practically right across the road from it."

"So now you know."

"Maybe I could talk to the people here."

"This one is up for sale, Caroline. See the sign?"

"Yes, but I mean the other place."

The car jarred forward, a perfect indication that my mother was growing irritable.

"I'll get this done very quickly," I promised, grab-

bing the tiny sound recorder I'd just bought with my
birthday savings.

"Please do."

Tucking it under my shirt, I got out and strode past a
garden of flowers to the front step of the small but very
pretty house. Even before I touched the buzzer, I caught
a fleeting glimpse of a narrow, very old, face peering at
me from behind a curtained window—though I couldn't
tell whether it belonged to a man or a woman. I rang,
but there was no answer.

"Caroline," my mother called from inside the car,
"let's go."

"There's someone home, Mom."

"They probably don't want intruders."

That was obviously the truth, but I still wasn't going
to give up. I rang again.

"Who is it?" a high-pitched voice asked through a
crack in the door.

"My name is Caroline Burns. And I'd like to speak
to you for just a minute."

"What do you want?"

"I'm a high school student, and my mother is with
me. . . ." What, I asked myself, could sound less threatening than that?

"Just a minute. . . ."

I heard one or two locks opening. The door swung
out a little ways upon a thick chain, and just behind it,
that tiny face peered at me again. "Yes, what is it?"

"Uh . . . I'm writing a column for my school paper.
This is it," I said, passing a copy through the door. "It
has my name on the inside page if you want to open
it."

"That's very nice, dear," said the woman. I could tell she was a little nervous.

I took a look around and saw that my mother was beginning to fidget. There wasn't much more time for diplomacy. "That's why I came here, because I heard about what happened to poor Mrs. Sorell and decided to do a story on the . . . uh . . . murder."

"Mrs. Sorell?" There was a tremble in her voice. "What has that to do with me?"

"It must have been very upsetting for you. I imagine you must have been home that night?"

Her hand fluttered on the door. "I don't want to talk about it. I am not well."

"I certainly understand that. After all, it was a terrible thing to happen so nearby."

"Yes, it was."

I decided to take a chance. "And especially for you, because you probably heard her screaming."

"Yes, it was horrible!"

I tried to control my excitement. "The police must have asked you a lot of questions."

Her voice was really trembling now. "No, they were very gentle and polite. And they told me I probably wouldn't have to go to court when they saw how upset I was. I always got so upset when that happened."

Her statement startled me. "You mean," I asked slowly, "you mean that you've heard screaming at other times from the Sorell house?"

"That's not what I said!" the woman said in a terrified voice. "That is not what I said! And don't you *ever* say that I did!"

And with that she slammed the door in my face.

"Caroline," said my mother as I came down the steps, "you can be one tough cookie."

"You think I did the wrong thing?"

"Not if I don't run into her tomorrow at the hospital."

"You mean that?"

She squeezed my hand. "No. I think you were fine. But she is old. And you might have been just a little gentler with her."

"You're right, you're right, you're right. But you know what?"

"What?"

"We've come up with something."

"Which is?"

"Agnes Sorell was a battered wife!"

Chapter 13

PAUL WAS INFURIATING as ever the next day when I played a tape for him of my interview with the old woman. "How did you get this?"

What a dumb question, I thought. I didn't even answer him.

"Did she know about your recording her? Did you tell her?"

"No, of course not."

He pushed it back at me. "Can't use it. That's a breach of ethics."

"What?"

"It is, but just to make you feel better," said Paul, "I don't see what this adds to the stew anyway. The woman denied your interpretation of it as soon as she said it. The words 'I always got so upset when that happened' can even refer to something entirely different."

"Paul," I said quietly, "you're driving me nuts."

"Good. That must mean I'm getting through to you. You say that Agnes Sorell was a battered wife. Fine, you could be right. Get me something to back it up that's not as sketchy as this."

"Like what—and where can I get it?"

"I don't know. You show me."

My mother called me from the hospital that afternoon to see how Paul reacted to my information.

"Well," she said, after I'd finished complaining, "he's certainly making you work for that story. I guess he's leaving it up to you to get all the information—the correct information. But I think I can help you, Caroline."

It was a long, hot, humid night. I couldn't fall asleep, although I was exhausted. My mother's room had the air conditioner, so finally I sagged into her empty bed, turned on the air, and passed out at last. I awoke in the middle of the night to find her sitting beside me with the light on.

"Caroline," she said, "I'm sorry to wake you, but I don't know if I'll be fit to get up and talk in the morning. I'm not at all sure how I feel about the rights and wrongs of doing this, and if it ever came out how you got this information, I would certainly lose my job. In fact, I don't know that I'd be able to work anywhere. So you must not tell anyone who gave it to you. Here."

I stared at a long list of medical notes in my mother's handwriting.

"What is this?"

"It simply occurred to me that if Mr. Sorell had been in the habit of beating his wife, then there were proba- bly times—especially at night—when she needed emergency treatment. So, during my break, I slipped into the medical records room.''

"These are her records?''

"Now, Caroline, I couldn't get to the Xerox machine to make exact copies—but I did manage to write down these dates and what she was treated for. This goes back about six years—and, really, these injuries—when you see them all together—so many of them, it's very hard to believe they didn't come from being beaten.''

"Mom, did she tell them at the hospital what had happened?''

"No, she said they were all caused by falls.''

"Then how can we—''

"Caroline, this woman would have had to have the worst sense of balance known to the human race.''

"But you don't know Paul. He is going to want something more.''

"He is just going to have to understand that battered wives don't usually tell the truth about these things. And especially not if their husbands have driven them to the hospital themselves and are standing right beside them.''

"Oh. Mom, you've taken such a risk for yourself, giving me all this information, but Paul Morris is only going to tell me to forget about it. I've got the facts, but these aren't photocopies of the real records and I can't bring in anybody to prove this!''

My mother thought it over. "If you feel you have to, then tell him who gave this list to you. He can talk to me and I'll confirm it. But he has to promise not to reveal my name. Not,'' she said, biting her lip, "that when someone finds out my daughter works for Channel 12, they won't put two and two together anyway.''

She fell silent again. "You can tell him that if it is absolutely necessary I will find a way to make the copies."

"I feel just horrible about putting you in a position like this."

"Once you see there's something you personally can do to keep an innocent man from being sent to prison, then it's hard *not* to be in that position. I just can't help feeling upset about revealing what's in confidential files. I keep having to remind myself that these are the *victim's* records and that she wouldn't want the wrong person to pay for what was done to her. Anyway, I've got to get some sleep."

I was scared and felt like I needed some company suddenly. "Mom," I said quietly. "Can I stay here with you?"

"If you don't snore," she smiled, "it would be very nice."

I wrapped my arms around her as soon as she climbed into bed and snuggled my way into sleep.

Chapter 14

BILL WAS VERY much in my rooting section. Together we hovered over Paul while he studied the list and listened to my new information. "Paul, there's the makings of something here," he said.

"The makings, yeah. But we're still way out on a limb. Her mother is in jeopardy."

Bill had an idea. "We could get an independent doctor to give us an opinion on what all these injuries add up to. And we—"

"Yes, I know what we can do," Paul muttered. "We could also go down a big legal sinkhole when the station gets sued."

"But if it works," cried Blake Thomas out of nowhere, "it would be a fabulous scoop!"

We all looked around. Blake had come in unnoticed and was standing there beaming at us.

"The way I look at it, when you put it all together,

including that recording Caroline got the other day of what that old woman said—''

Paul raised a bushy eyebrow. "How did *you* hear about that?"

"Oh, I've got my ways."

"Yeah, I can see that." Paul studied him for a moment. "You want it?"

"Damn straight! It's right up my alley! It's got all my juices going."

"Wait a minute," I protested. "This is Barbara's story!"

"That," said Blake coolly, "is not up to you. Look Paul, Barbara walked away from this one. She dropped the ball here."

"Not so." Bill jumped in. "It was a normal wrap-up."

"I'm sorry, that doesn't sit right with me. Here is an inexperienced young kid who senses there's something more to the story. Why didn't *Barbara* turn over that first rock and begin to see the little worms wriggling under it?"

"You tell me," said Paul.

"Because her body's here—but her soul is up at network! But I'm a rock bottom, tell-it-like-it-is, working broadcast reporter. Paul, I've got the background for this. I've got a lot of seniority here. . . ."

I raced away for the editing booth where I knew I'd find Barbara working on some feature with Don. "Come back in the newsroom. Blake is trying to take your story from you."

Barbara looked up and gave me a small smile. "Thank you for telling me, Caroline, but he can take any story he wants. I really don't care."

"It's about the Sorell murder. I found out that Mr.

Sorell had been badly beating his wife for years. She'd been going to the hospital.''

"*You* found out?''

"Yes. And neither the police nor Brown's lawyer did anything about checking into Willy Brown's story.''

"What story?''

"She blamed her husband for that beating. She told it to him when he went into the house to help her. That was just before he heard someone drive away.''

"Wait a minute!'' She stood up. "Where did you get all this? Did *you* speak to Brown?''

"Yes.''

"When?''

"Right after you left the courthouse.''

"Then I really don't understand.'' A very surprised look crossed her face. "Why did you wait all this time to tell me? What were you trying to do—show me up?''

"No!''

"Take it easy, Barb. She's coming to tell you now.''

"Yes, but that happened *days* ago.''

"Barbara, I tried to tell you right away but you were too busy. And then Paul didn't think it was anything for Channel 12 until I came up with more.'' By now there were tears in my eyes. "You were very unfair!''

"Oh, I was?''

"Yes!''

"Well . . . maybe you're right. Maybe I was, and still am.'' She fell silent, then all at once shook her head as if to clear it. "Oh boy. So it's happening to me. I've gone into the same kind of paranoia they used to hit *me* with when I was starting out. Then *I* was the one scaring people with how eager and Johnny-on-the-spot I was. Caroline, I'm sorry. I'll make it up to you.''

She strode past me, heading for the newsroom, and I followed—feeling better than I had for some time. "Paul," she said quietly but firmly as she came up to his desk, "you're not thinking, I hope, of reassigning my story?"

"There aren't any property rights in a newsroom," he answered her carefully. "And Blake here has had years of background covering crime beats for the papers and TV. He knows how to go about it, who to talk to—and where the bones are buried."

"Any other reasons, Paul?"

"Yep. There is some truth in the notion that you just played this one by the numbers. . . ."

"That's exactly why this is so important to me. Paul."

"Oh?" said Blake, "and not because you belatedly smell a big one, Barbara?"

"Yes, Blake, that's part of it, too."

"I think," Paul grumbled, "I'm just going to forget the whole thing. All of you guys may be touting this as a Pulitzer Prize-winner, but as far as I'm concerned it's still a long shot . . . and it's going to tie up too much time and talent. On top of that, I am not going to see another battle royal between you two. So out it goes."

"No, you can't!" I shouted. "You just can't!"

"Caroline, don't tell me what I can or cannot do."

"All right!" Barbara snapped angrily. "Blake can have it. I'm out of it. If this is the only chance a man who could be innocent might have of getting off death row, then I'm not going to stand in the way of it. Or of Caroline's story either. But I do expect *her* to get some credit for it. And, Paul, I still want you to know that I am angry about all this."

Wearily Paul turned to Blake, saying, "Now we just had one noble gesture. How would you like to take the high road yourself and do the right thing by Barbara?"

"First of all," Blake shot back, "she's deliberately playing the martyr. This is a ploy. And secondly, the days of male chivalry went out long ago. I'm senior newsperson here and I put in the first bid on this."

Paul gave off a deep sigh. "I think I am going to smoke now. Who's got a light?"

"Here." Bill struck a match, but at the same time yanked the cigarette away from Paul's mouth.

"Thanks, buddy," Paul said dryly. "Okay, decision time. It's yours, Barb. But no more sulking."

"That's a promise," she said with a grin. "Caroline, do you still want to work with me after all we've *not* been through?"

"Very much."

She put her arm around my shoulders and gave me a big smile. "Well, let's get started!"

Chapter 15

I WAITED AROUND until after the evening broadcast. Then Barbara and I drove out to the farm area to find the missing witness. No one on any of the other farms we went to seemed to know George Blackwell—or would admit it if they did.

"What we have here," Barbara said at last, "are a lot of frightened people. These people figure that, no matter what we tell them we're trying to do, we all still work for someone."

"You mean Mr. Sorell?" I asked.

"I mean *all* the Mr. Sorells who are the authority figures in their lives. They don't really think that anyone who's got the power to change anything will give a migrant worker with no roots and no money an even break. So if there *is* a George Blackwell around, why get him into trouble along with Willy Brown?"

We sat in Barbara's car, trying to figure out what to

do next. "I'm going to take you home—and then I'm going to make a call."

"Who to?" I wanted to know.

She started the car. "A source. Someone to give me an idea about what we're dealing with here. I want to know more about Benjamin Sorell."

"Why can't I go along?"

"Doesn't your mother want you home by now?"

"She's still working."

"Well, if I can meet with this person, I'm not sure he'd like me to bring anyone else along."

"Can't I just wait nearby somewhere?"

She gave me a smile. "Persistent, aren't you?"

I gave her a smile back.

They met in a little restaurant. A dignified man in an immaculate business suit came in and sat down at our table as if he were a regular customer—although the impression I got somehow was that he owned the place.

"Max," she said, after he actually kissed her hand, "meet my . . . fellow journalist, Caroline Burns."

"My pleasure," he said, kissing my hand, too.

"Tell me about Benjamin Sorell. Is he a more important man than one might expect from his job as county treasurer?"

"What are you asking?"

Barbara planted her elbows on the table and her chin on her cupped hands. "Does he, for example, carry a good deal of influence in this state with . . . say, district attorneys, police captains . . . trial judges . . .?"

Max smiled. "My darling, all I can say is that Benjamin Sorell is one of the nicest—and most generous—men in the world. And you can quote me on that."

"This is all off the record, Max, as usual. So do you want to elaborate?"

"Ask anyone. He is very articulate . . . and very soft-spoken. A fine man."

"Are people afraid of him?" I put in.

Max ignored my question. I suddenly felt like Barbara was right in saying I shouldn't come.

Barbara went smoothly along. "Tell me about his . . . generosity."

"Ben gives to all the charities." He smiled again.

"And political campaigns?"

"But of course."

"He doesn't seem all that rich."

"Not everyone displays their wealth, my dear."

"Is it his own money he contributes?"

"As usual," said Max, giving her an admiring stare, "you ask a very perceptive question. Benjamin Sorell is a man of great human . . . friendliness. And what he does is bring together those who need the money and those who wish to donate . . . or invest it."

"He's a go-between."

Max sat back. "Ah, yes."

"You mentioned investments. What sort?"

"Oh . . . any business, Barbara. Anything, for instance, from helping put together a lending company . . . to possibly the purchase of a television station."

"Then what are you saying?"

"Simply," he murmured, rising to his feet, "that I would look into that if I intended to describe the gentleman over the air as anything but . . . one of the nicest men in the world." There was a long pause.

"Thank you," Barbara said softly. "Warning received."

"Oh? Did I warn anyone?" A friendly wave, and he was gone.

We sat together silently for a long while. "So," I said, "where does that leave us?"

"As two newswomen," she answered with a tough little grin, "who are out to get our story."

"Great!"

The phone was ringing when Barbara dropped me off, but by the time I got to the door it had stopped. It must be Helen, I thought, remembering that I owed her a call from the day before. I dialed her number.

"It's me," I said. "I'm really sorry I didn't call to find out what happened with Moe, but yesterday I came home and just flopped. Honestly, this is getting to be an around-the-clock thing. What's happened? Did you finally hear from him?"

"No, I went over there myself."

"Oh, Helen, you didn't!"

"I had to. Please don't make me feel like any more of a fool."

"Okay, so what happened?"

"I won't even go into it. He was so nasty. But believe me, I'm glad I did it. He is such a worm. I am so relieved that I have finally seen through him—you have no idea!"

"You mean you're free of all this?"

"I sure am! I tell you, I feel like I've come out of the end of a long tunnel. It's like I was in the dark, not knowing what was happening to me. Not having any control at all over my life. I can't tell you how important it is to know you have some kind of control!"

"That's wonderful," I said.

"Then how come you don't *sound* so happy for me?"

"I just want to be sure that you mean it. And that you don't get yourself in another situation like this." I knew full well that before the summer ended, Helen would have at least one more tragic romantic encounter.

"Who says I don't mean it?" she demanded.

"It's just that you're sounding a little bit—"

"What?"

"I don't know—upset maybe."

"Well, wouldn't you be upset," she screamed, "if he said he just wanted *you* to leave him alone!"

"Oh, Helen, how could he? I hope you really let him have it."

"I sure did! I gave him a bloody nose!"

"You *socked* him?"

"No! I took off my shoe and hit him with that!" She burst into tears.

"It's okay. Just keep crying." I felt bad for Helen. I wished she wouldn't put herself in these situations and that I had more time to spend with her. What she really needed was someone to like her for herself, and to stop pushing so much when someone showed the slightest bit of interest.

"Can you come over?" she finally sobbed in a tiny voice.

"Helen, I can't. We'd be up all night talking—and I'm meeting Barbara in the morning to—"

"On Saturday?"

"Yes! She's coming in on her own time—and we're working on the Willy Brown story together!"

"Really?"

"Really!"

"Oh well . . . I mean, that's so important, if you can come up with something."

"I wish I could say we're getting somewhere with our search for that witness. It's very hard—"

"That doesn't matter. You're trying. That's what counts."

"Look, I'll come over tomorrow night. Will that be all right?"

"You promise? You absolutely promise?"

"Yes! Of course I promise. I'm your best friend, right?"

"Right." She sniffled. "See you then."

"See you then."

Chapter 16

BARBARA PICKED ME UP bright and early the next morning.

"What are we going to do now?" I asked as I climbed in the car.

"You told me yesterday that one of the two houses across from the Sorells' place was up for sale?"

"Yes, there was a sign."

"Well, neither Don nor I recall the sign being out there the day we went to cover the murder. I got to thinking about that last night. It occurred to me what a coincidence it was that the police just happened to be driving nearby when Brown was trying to get away from the place. Of course it's possible, but—"

"You think the owner of the house called them?"

"Let's look at it a moment as if someone had. Do you think that old lady you spoke to would have been the one to do it?"

"I don't think so. She seemed too frightened to call the police."

"Then it would have to have been the one other neighbor. And, since it took time for the cops to get there, then the call must have been made while the beating was still going on."

"What I don't get, Barbara, is why the police captain you interviewed didn't simply tell the truth about someone calling in?"

"He might have been mistaken. But let's assume for a minute he was hiding something. What would that be?"

"I don't know."

"Caroline, think about it. What would have happened if he hadn't lied? What would I and the other reporters have done right away?"

I caught on. "You would have interviewed the person who made the call. And you might have found out that he could have phoned the police to come there other times, too!"

"Which means?"

"That they knew all along Mr. Sorell was a man who beat his wife!"

"So at the very least, there would have had to be a real investigation of Benjamin Sorell before Brown was charged. I can tell you that never happened. What we're talking about here," she said with a delighted grin, "is a nice thick cover-up!"

"But why didn't the person who made the call say something?"

"In this less-than-perfect world, Caroline, maybe that person saw the police captain lying on television and decided it would be a trifle safer not to volunteer any more information.''

"Wouldn't Paul call this an awful lof of *ifs*?''

"He sure would,'' she laughed. "So let's hope that our caller isn't harder to find than Mr. Blackwell.''

We drove out to Ben Sorell's neighborhood, and Barbara rang the bell at the old woman's house.

"Who is it?'' came that same high voice.

"I'm Barbara Richie from Channel 12.''

"Who?'' The door didn't open at all this time.

"Barbara Richie.''

"From the television?''

"Yes.''

"Please go away. I'm not feeling well.''

"I understand that—and I just wanted to apologize to you for our having upset you yesterday. You know,'' she said, gazing around. "You have one of the nicest gardens I've ever seen. And you even have *black* roses. That's very unusual.''

The door opened a crack and the old lady's face appeared behind the chain. "The garden really isn't very good at all this year. I just wasn't up to much planting. And the tulips hardly came up. Last year it was so much nicer with the azaleas and tulips to balance the color.''

The woman opened the door entirely and stepped outside in her housecoat. "If you come inside, I can show you photographs of how it always used to look.''

"That's awfully nice of you, but I don't want to keep you.''

"That's all right. I have plenty of time—and I love to watch you on television. Though I do turn off the sound when the news is so bad. But you have to promise me not to talk about that terrible case. It's made me very ill."

"I promise. We both promise," Barbara said as we all stepped inside. "Because I can imagine how it must be for *you*, if that gentleman next door felt he had to move away."

"Oh, don't ask. Mr. Timmerman was very upset. This whole thing has been simply terrible for him. Wait, I'll get my album."

"Barbara," I said, "I just wish I could have been this subtle."

"Compliments later. Let's find out who made that call, if there was one."

"I can't believe it would have been her."

"You can't ever tell about these things. I've had a lot of surprises in my life."

Speaking of surprises, the old lady came back carrying a book that was almost as big as she was. "Here it is," she said. "My little album."

As patiently as we could manage, Barbara and I sipped tea, and I leafed through the book.

"Well, now," she said when we were through, "what can I do for you?"

"I really do love your flowers," Barbara declared.

"Well, I hope so. Have some butter cookies—and I won't hold you here any longer."

"Would it upset you if I asked you what you think of Mr. Sorell?"

"He's a mean man—and I won't say anything further than that."

"Was Mrs. Sorell a nice person?"

"Oh, she was so sweet. Such a nice woman. And

always making excuses for him . . . but I won't go into any of that.''

"How did Mr. Timmerman get along with the Sorells?''

"Mr. Timmerman would never fight with anybody. That's why he suffered so much from hearing those quarrels. I told him to turn up his television set like I did, but he didn't even have a television. He read a lot.''

Barbara put down her teacup and wiped her lips with a napkin. If I were a man I probably would have called the police, too, when those things happened.''

"Well, after a few years it got to be so terrible. But then the police wouldn't do anything about it. He'd call them, but the police would just come out and turn around and go away again. And then, of course, Mr. Sorell would get so mad at Mr. Timmerman afterwards.''

"Really?''

"Oh, yes.''

"Then why didn't Mr. Timmerman do something about that?''

"You can't do anything with that man. Everyone kowtows to him. We were both so sure that it was *he*—''

Barbara and I sat there hanging on her next words, but she checked herself.

"I really am very tired now. And I do hope you won't say anything about our conversation to anyone.''

"I understand,'' Barbara said, rising from the table. "You have to live here. At least Mr. Timmerman had somewhere he could move to.''

"That's right. My family is all gone. But he has a brother in Cooperville. I'm really sorry I wasn't helpful to you. But you know, I just can't be involved.''

"Thank you very much anyway." We got up to go.

"You're welcome, I'm sure."

"So far, so frustrating," Barbara murmured as we walked to the car. "We're learning a lot, but we still have nothing we can put on television. And short of coming up with George Blackwell, we've got to nail down a probably very frightened Mr. Timmerman, just to raise the issue of a fair trial."

"So off we race to Cooperville?"

"You just read my speedometer."

It was quite a drive, but at least we had no trouble finding the house once we got there—there was only one Timmerman in the directory. The place was a lot different from the one on sale back in Ridgewood Park, being even smaller and made of logs. Anyway, no one was home. We camped in the car until sunset— and finally, two heavyset men showed up carrying fishing rods and those bags you carry fish in. We stepped out of the car and walked toward them.

"Mr. Timmerman?"

"Yes?" They had both answered at once, and with the same smile. Barbara looked from one to the other. "I think I'm having double vision. I'm Barbara Richie. And this is—"

The smile faded from one of the men's faces. "I wondered where I knew you from." He gestured to his brother. "This lady does the news on television."

"You're hiding things from me, Jim. I thought you didn't have a set."

"There's one at the tavern where I eat." He turned back to Barbara and gazed at her thoughtfully. But I could see that she was waiting too—and she deliberately let the silence linger.

"You're putting me on the spot, you know," he finally said in a low, troubled voice.

"Yes, I know."

He took a deep breath. "What is it you know?"

"That you called the police on the day of the murder."

"What makes you say I did?"

"It . . . fits together."

He nodded. "Do you want to come into the house?"

"Yes, please."

We took our seats around a small table.

"Mr. Timmerman," Barbara began. "I have a tape recorder here to get your statement down correctly. So please don't feel intimidated by it." She plunked it on the table. "And also there's a television camera in my car."

"I'd rather you didn't use any of them."

"Well, it might be very important."

"Let's just talk."

"All right." She fell silent and began to wait again.

"The truth of the matter is that I feel a little ashamed."

"Why is that?" she asked softly.

"No one can be proud of letting their fears drive them into hiding."

"Good Lord, Jim!" his brother cut in impatiently. "How can you call it hiding when these people found you easy as pie? You don't like the situation and you changed it. That's all it was."

"What were you afraid of, Mr. Timmerman?"

"What? I can't answer that directly. . . ."

"Did anyone threaten you?"

"In words, you mean?"

"In any way?"

He pressed his hands together. "That's something I can't be sure of. . . ."

Barbara was getting frustrated. "I understand," she began, "that Mr. Sorell has made threatening remarks to you in the past."

"How did you find that out?" He tossed a quick, worried glance at her.

"Your neighbor."

"I just wish she hadn't said anything."

"But it's true, isn't it?"

"Yes, it is," he answered nervously. "But just let me say this. The fact that Ben Sorell has beaten his wife on other times does *not* make him guilty of it *this* time! In fact, I don't know who did it."

"Why don't you tell us, then, what you did see and hear."

"See? I saw nothing. I was sitting by my open window, dozing over a book, when I heard her screams. To be perfectly honest, I shut the window and did everything I could to put it out of my mind. But they were terrible—and they just grew worse. They went on and on. And even though Agnes—Mrs. Sorell—had begged and pleaded with me several times before never to call the police again, I got so frightened for her that I did telephone them."

"And what did you say?"

"You must come right away, please. Mr. Sorell's beating his wife terribly!"

Barbara leaned forward. "Who did you tell that to?"

"I don't know which officer answered the phone."

"But how did you know who was beating her this time. Did you hear Mr. Sorell's voice, too?"

Timmerman stood up. "No. I just assumed it was him. I may very well have been incorrect."

I knew I wasn't supposed to butt in. Barbara was conducting this—those were the rules. I asked my question anyway. "Did you hear anyone else's voice? I mean, besides Mrs. Sorell's?"

"No, I did not. If I had, I wouldn't have phoned to say Sorell was doing it again."

"Did you overhear anything else?" Barbara asked.

"No, why?"

"I was wondering if you happened to hear a car drive away from the house?"

"I did hear a car, but I don't know what that has to do with anything."

"Willy Brown didn't have a car, Mr. Timmerman. He was the first seen after the murder, walking on the road."

"The car could, I suppose, have been coming from farther down the road."

"Was it, Jim?" his brother asked softly.

Jim Timmerman stared down at his hands. "No. I could hear it being started up—there was some trouble with it. And then I could hear gravel from the driveway flying all over. It was from there." He fell silent.

"Jim," said his brother, "this is turning my stomach." He gazed at us. "My brother is giving you the impression that, after he called the police, he washed his hands and walked away from it. It's just not true. He was very concerned about this man, Willy Brown—and whether there was fair play here."

"Concerned?" his twin snorted. "I kept reading the papers every day—hoping that the man would confess and I wouldn't be in the middle of it."

"But he didn't. And tell her what you *did* do about contacting that lawyer who was put on to defend the man. What was his name?"

"Giezel. Yes, I spoke to him. I'd been mulling over the fact that nobody tried to contact me, since I'd called the police. I got to thinking that Brown's lawyer should at least be told about the other beatings."

"Was it by phone?" I suddenly asked. He answered me with a nod. I glanced at Barbara. She was grinning at me. "And then what?"

"Well, Giezel asked me to come to his office—which I did that evening."

"Go on."

"I told him everything about those other times and what I knew about that night."

"Including calling the police, hearing her screams, and the car?"

"Yes, everything."

"What did he say?"

"He said it was all very important. In fact, he took it all down while I talked and made me sign what he wrote."

"Did he give you a copy?" Barbara broke in to ask.

"I did ask for one, but he said his photocopy machine was broken. He would mail me one. I never got it—and he never asked me to come to the courthouse later when the trial began."

"Didn't you think there was something strange about that?" I said, going back to my questioning.

"Yes, but then I asked myself, who am I to tell a lawyer what to do."

"Tell them about the silent calls, Jim," his brother put in.

"Yes." Mr. Timmerman sighed. "That had something to do with it, too. A lot." He looked away from us.

We waited.

"Right after I saw Giezel," he began again, "a day later, I started to get strange phone calls. Whoever was on the other end of the line—they just stayed there, saying nothing to my hellos, until I'd hang up."

Remembering that I had done things like that myself in my childhood, I asked if he didn't think they were only prank calls.

He shook his head. "It just didn't feel that way. And I've got an unlisted number."

"Did you give your number," Barbara asked, "to Mr. Giezel?"

"Yes. And to the police."

He said that in such a way that right away I immediately asked, "Do you suspect the police?"

He shrugged. "What good is suspecting?"

Barbara leaned forward. "Do you happen to know if Ben Sorell and the Ridgewood Park police captain are well acquainted?"

Mr. Timmerman began to study his hands again. "I've seen them together a number of times. Maybe about once a month Captain Burke goes over there with some other people."

"Do you know who they are?" Barbara asked.

"No . . ." His voice trailed off.

This was the time for Barbara to nail things down or we would lose the interview. "Mr. Timmerman, there is no question but that you could be sticking your neck out by coming forward now. I won't pretend to you that it is the entirely safe thing to do. But I will say that if

Channel 12 pushes this thing into the open, we will come at them from several directions at once. And I think you agree that at the very least, Willy Brown should have the right to a fairer trial for his life than the one he received.''

"When you live across the road from a man who gets away with as much as Ben Sorell does," he said, hesitating, "you get to believe he has everyone in his pocket.''

"He doesn't have us," Barbara assured him. "I would like to go on record with what you know and put this on videotape. It's really the only way we can move toward getting justice here. What do you say?"

He turned to his brother. "Martin?"

"Your decision," he said, getting up and walking to the sink with his catch. "I just cook fish."

Jim Timmerman gave a little smile. "He cooks fish and I go on television.''

My head was still buzzing when I got home. It was late, but I lay awake just tasting in my mind everything that had happened that day, every word, every moment. Barbara had warned me that there was a lot more to be done—and we would have to see what Paul said on Monday—but I was sure that now we were on our way to saving Willy Brown.

And she and I were doing it together—that was the best part of it!

I must have fallen asleep before my mother came dragging home from work, because I didn't hear her come in. This time she didn't wake me, and we both slept blissfully until noon.

We were having breakfast together out on the porch

when I suddenly remembered my promise to Helen and jumped to my feet. "Oh no! I was supposed to sleep over at Helen's last night!"

"She'll survive."

"No, she won't!" And I bolted into the house.

I unfortunately got her father on the line. He told me that Helen had tried to reach me all day yesterday and that she was very upset. Finally he ended with. "Frankly, Caroline, you let her down."

I could hear his wife shushing him in the background, but he went on to remind me that I was the one teenager they had always trusted to set a good example for Helen, that they had practically considered me as one of the family—so why hadn't I at least called last night?

"Mr. Bauer, I'm really very sorry. But can I just talk to her, please?"

"No, you can't talk to her; she's not here."

"Can you tell me where she is, please?" I asked in a pleading little squeak.

Helen's father seemed to regain *his* composure and answered in a calm voice, "You could give a call to her aunt's house in Connecticut. We put her on the 9:30 bus this morning."

"Could you give me the number?"

As soon as we ended the conversation, I dialed Helen's aunt. There was no answer. I tried calling again about an hour later, and four or five times after that. When I finally did get through that evening, Helen wasn't even there.

"My television is being repaired," her aunt explained, "so after we left my senior citizen's meeting, I dropped her off at the movies. They're showing *Dr. Zhivago* again. I thought it might cheer her up.''

I begged her several times to have Helen call me the moment she came in. "I will," she promised, and hung up. Everything else went out the window. My mother and I canceled our plans for the beach so I could stick by the phone, but Helen never called me back. At about ten, I tried again and the aunt answered.

"I'm sorry, dear, but Helen doesn't want to talk to you."

"I know she's mad at me. Only please ask her to get on and I'll explain."

Helen's aunt put the phone down, then came back a few moments later. "I'm very sorry, but she won't speak to you. . . ."

"Get on with your own life," my mother told me after I hung up. "Helen has to learn to help herself."

"But, Mom, I let her down."

"We all do it once in a while."

But that didn't make me feel any better.

Chapter 17

MONDAY STARTED MY last week at Channel 12, and all of my expectations of a glorious finish were making me impatient with the newsroom chores I'd been doing since 6:00 A.M. Barbara, too, was on edge. She had shown Paul and Dave Hammersmith the footage of our interview with Jim Timmerman. Now we were both waiting for an endless private conference between our two bosses to come to an end.

"What's going on?" she asked when Paul finally emerged from the news manager's office. "I feel like I've been sitting on an unhatched egg all morning."

"Barbara, let's go into your room where we can talk," Paul said.

"Uh-oh."

"Not as bad as you think," he replied, leading her by the arm. But when I got up to follow, he waved me away.

"She goes, too. Caroline worked hard on this. I want her in on everything with me."

"Won't argue it," he agreed with a sigh.

As soon as I'd shut the door behind me, Paul turned to us. "Bottom line, you two. is this. And it's not negotiable. That was great stuff, but we can't go on the air with it now."

Barbara's eyes grew wide. "Why not!"

"Because the station could be hit with a bunch of libel suits, that's why. You've got Sorell made out the battering husband of all time, and Willy Brown's lawyer, Giezel, practically throwing the case. Suppose we can't prove it?"

"I don't understand this," Barbara snapped. "These aren't *our* charges. *Other* people are making these statements. We are only presenting the news."

"Come on, that trial is over. We're *making* the news here."

"Are we dropping it then?" I suddenly asked.

Paul waggled a finger at me. "I didn't say that. What I want is more."

"More what?" Barbara demanded.

"More facts. Evidence. Back-up."

"Like what?"

"Like tie-ins between this lawyer and Sorell. How do we know there is one? Maybe there isn't? Like business arrangements—with judges, cops, the DA—*something*. Even if it's off the record, it's a back-up."

"You realize how much you're asking?"

"You don't want to do all that? Then get me this George Blackwell. If he pans out, that could set off the whole shooting match right there."

"I think," said Barbara, "that we first have to go on

the air with some of this just to make him feel that he *can* come out and talk to us."

"Then we're back to what I said." Paul headed for the door. "Get me more!"

The rest of the day was frustrating. Barbara went out looking for George Blackwell—"Just to give it the college try"—while I got dumped at the Central Public Library in front of a mountain of back issues of the *Daily Express,* our only local newspaper. It wasn't as if I was looking for something in particular—just anything that could connect the people we were investigating. Do you know how many issues you have to slosh through when you go back five years on a paper that publishes every day? My eyes were blurring by the time she came back for me.

"I've got nothing," she said. "What have you got?"

"Nothing really, just how prominent he is. Well, there was a lawsuit about some real estate development he was putting together. Sorell won."

"Who was his lawyer?"

I read from the photocopy I had made of the article. "Amos Walgren."

The next day I returned to the library to go back another few years in the *Express.* By this time, I noticed that there had been a second newspaper in those days, *The Herald-Ledger*. It was in that paper I came across an article about Willy Brown's lawyer.

I couldn't wait to get a hold of Barbara later, before the evening broadcast. "Guess what?"

"What?"

"In 1976, Adam Giezel was almost disbarred because they said he'd embezzled money from the widow

of one of his clients. Want to know who was his lawyer
and got him off with only a bawling out?''

"I can feel it coming.''

"Amos Walgren.''

"Shall I tell *you* something about Amos Walgren?''
Barbara added.

"What?''

"He is the father-in-law of a certain Judge Kappel.''

This confused me. I'd never even heard of this Kappel.
"But Barbara, he wasn't the judge who tried the case.''

"But Caroline, he *was* the judge who signed the
order to give Willy Brown that terrible lawyer. And the
court clerk tells me it's unusual for that judge to have
been the one who did it.''

From the look on her face I could tell we were
cooking. "Do we have enough now?''

"We will just as soon as I have my interview on
camera with Mr. Adam Giezel.''

"Can you really get one?''

"Does a lawyer want free publicity?''

"But what if he already knows what we're up to?''

"We just have to hope he doesn't, and move fast.''

Two minutes later she had him on the phone. "Hello?
Mr. Giezel? I see you're one of those people who stay
late at the office. Glad I reached you. This is Barbara
Richie of Channel 12 News. . . .

"Yes, that's right. Nice to talk to you again. Well,
I'm doing a story on criminal justice—and I was im-
pressed by your handling of the Brown case. . . .

"I know, but you can't win them all, can you? Anyway
I'd love to have your comments for the benefit of our
audience.

"What? . . . Oh yes, there's one other—very prominent—attorney we may interview, but he would come later. . . . You would? Marvelous. How about tonight? . . . Well, you know—deadlines, deadlines. Would eight o'clock at your office do? . . . That's fine.'' She hung up.

We arrived fifteen minutes earlier than expected at Giezel's office. Barbara wanted to give him as little time as possible to change his mind. As we walked across the downstairs lobby, I spotted a plaque on the wall and read, ''This property owned and managed by Amos Walgren Associates.'' I read it again. ''Barbara, look.''

''Don, shoot that.''

''You got it.''

''Could that mean anything to us?'' I asked as we stepped into the elevator.

''Something to look into, maybe. . . .''

We got out on the third floor and found the office. Giezel was waiting for us in the reception room just inside, and it was easy to see he was already having second thoughts.

''You know, folks, I'm really not the world's biggest expert on the criminal law system.''

''Oh, I don't know,'' I replied. ''At the courthouse I heard a lot of other lawyers talking about you. They thought you did a very unusual job.''

''Really? Well, where do you want me to be while we do this?''

Barbara looked around. ''How about your library, among all your law books.''

''I really don't have one.'' He sort of laughed. ''Just a few volumes. I like to use the one in the courthouse;

I'm always there anyhow. Let's go into my private office. And you can shoot me at my desk.''

"With pleasure."

"What kind of questions are you going to ask me?" he said, taking a seat while Don set up.

"The first ones," Barbara told him, "should make you feel more relaxed."

"Good, good."

When Don was ready to roll, she began by facing the camera and introducing Giezel as the lawyer who had been appointed by the court to defend Willy Brown in "the celebrated murder case."

He was smiling as she turned to him. "Mr. Giezel. Under our American system of law, isn't it true that a defendant is always considered innocent until proven guilty?"

"Yes, of course."

"In other words, a defendant doesn't have to testify and defend himself? It's up to the other side to prove the case against him?"

"Absolutely."

"But on the other hand, suppose he does have some evidence that would prove his innocence? Wouldn't it be a good idea for the defense to somehow bring that out in front of the jury?"

"Certainly."

"In that case," Barbara said coolly, "why didn't you have Willy Brown tell the jury that before she collapsed on the kitchen floor, Mrs. Sorell blamed her own husband for the beating that killed her?"

I've never seen what a cornered rat looks like, but in my imagination it must have been something like the way Mr. Giezel looked at that moment. "I . . . don't know where you got that information, Ms. Richie."

"From Mr. Brown himself, in an interview one of our staff had with him after the verdict."

He drew himself up in what I think was supposed to be a dignified manner. "I believe we are discussing the system of criminal justice."

"We are."

"Well then, it was my decision not to put him on the stand to testify. But since you asked, I don't think Brown would have helped his defense, making that kind of an accusation. There is always a lot of sympathy for a bereaved husband."

"Even for one who was in the habit of beating his wife?"

"I beg your pardon?"

"Why didn't you call Mr. Timmerman to testify to those beatings?"

"Who?"

"James Timmerman, the neighbor of the Sorells who says he met with you and told you the police knew about these incidents. He says he also told you that on the night of the murder, he heard Agnes Sorell screaming and a car leaving their driveway. Willy Brown, as we all know, was on foot."

I held my breath. Oh boy! She's got him now I thought. He glanced at the camera, then back to Barbara, before he managed to pull together a controlled smile. Mr. Giezel shook his head and said, "This is somewhat unpleasant to say, Ms. Richie, especially before the thousands of people who are going to be looking at this. But since you bring it up, I will have to tell you that Mr. Timmerman came to me with his 'story' and seemed very . . . well, unstable. It was very clear to me that he could hurt our case more than help it. I could not, in good conscience, use that man as a witness for Brown without further evidence.''

"To get that evidence, did you check the records in Central Hospital to see if Mrs. Sorell had been treated for injuries on some of the days he says there were beatings?"

"Yes," Mr. Giezel said stiffly. "As a matter of fact I did. But there was nothing in them that said she claimed to be a victim of physical abuse."

"Did you have a medical doctor from outside the hospital look at them?"

"Yes, I did."

"Who?"

He showed his teeth in another, slightly larger, smile. "This is begining to feel like a cross-examination, Ms. Richie. You should have been a lawyer."

"Thank you. Who was he?"

"Just take my word for it."

"I see. What did he tell you?"

"That her falls were probably due to a middle ear problem which affected her balance."

"All *thirteen* of them?"

"That's what he said."

"Did you check into the police station records to learn how many times they had been to the Sorell house because of Mr. Timmerman's calls?"

"I think Mr. Timmerman went a little overboard on that one, too."

"But did you check?"

"In our state, Ms. Richie, the prosecutor is supposed to bring out such information in the interests of justice."

"But if he doesn't, then isn't it your job to dig it out?"

"Look, you have to understand, Ms. Richie, that lawyers have many cases to attend to at the same time. And, although the state pays to defend someone who can't afford private counsel, they don't give you the kind of money that permits a long, drawn-out—"

"Mr. Giezel," Barbara interrupted. "The lawyer who defended you in 1976 against your disbarment for embezzlement of a client's money is Mr. Sorell's business partner—and also your present landlord. And isn't he, as well, the father-in-law of the judge who put you on the Willy Brown case?"

"I don't," he said shakily, "think that has anything to do with—"

"What's your connection with Amos Walgren, Mr. Giezel?"

Giezel jumped up. "I did not ask to be put on as Brown's lawyer. The judge who appointed me had every right to do so, since he conducted the arraignment. I had no idea *whose* son-in-law he was. I was never disbarred or convicted of embezzlement. There was just an error in the bookkeeping which was straightened out. There is no crime in owing rent to your landlord. And this, I think, has gone far enough!"

"Thank you so much for a very enlightening interview," Barbara said as she rose.

We waited to say anything to each other until we were out of the building.

"Well," Barbara asked us, "what do you think? Did I nail him or did he wriggle out?"

"The man," Don answered slowly, "managed to come up with an answer for everything."

She halted beside the van. "But Don, no matter how he twisted things, it still is obvious that this lawyer was negligent and sloppy all over the place. And at the very least, there's the Walgren stuff. That was just too much of a connection to Sorell."

"I'm sure Paul will say that anything to do with Walgren will have to be edited out of our tape."

"Oh brother."

"Facts of life. Walgren's the lawyer for our station. You don't bite the hand that may be part of your own arm unless you absolutely can't help it. . . . At least that's how Dave is going to see it."

Barbara nodded. "He'll say there's not enough to go with—and Paul will agree with him."

"So where are we?" I demanded.

"That's easy to answer." Barbara laid her arm over my shoulder. "Still looking for *more*."

Chapter 18

UNFORTUNATELY, FRIDAY TURNED up before the "more" that we needed. Suddenly it was my last day at the station. Barbara and Don made a plea to keep me on—I was a volunteer anyway—but the answer was no. It had something to do, Dave Hammersmith said, with insurance coverage and company regulations. Also the fact that there was another intern coming in—from a college this time.

Paul shook my hand. "So long, Caroline. I'm going to miss you." Then, without missing a beat, he wheeled around and went straight off to the two-way to answer a reporter's call in.

Don said, "I'll be seeing you. And give your mother a hello from me."

Bill gave me a hug, and Barbara took me out to dinner. It all felt very strange, everything coming to an end like this. I was kind of numb.

"Don't worry about Willy Brown," Barbara promised me. "I'll keep at it even if I have to go on the air to plead for help in finding this George Blackwell. We'll be in touch."

I nodded and hugged her, and shook her hand, and even took a seven dollar cab ride home. It was a lot of money, but I couldn't help it. Nobody wants to cry all over a bus.

Chapter 19

MY MOTHER HAD arranged her vacation time to start just when I got through at Channel 12. She's a great hiker, so we tossed on our backpacks and went into the mountains for a few days. The weather was perfect, and the bugs hardly bothered us. We slept in our bags without ever pitching our tent, spending hours picking out the constellations—with the help of a book that we'd bought.

But the Willy Brown case never really left my mind— and the moment we got home on Monday I called the station to see how the investigation was going.

The new intern who answered didn't seem to know anything about it, so I asked if I could speak to Barbara.

"She's not here. Can I take a message?"

"Let me talk to Paul."

There was a quick click, and he came on. "What's up?"

"Nothing. I just wanted to know about the Brown—"

"Still working in it. Anything else?"

"No."

"Gotta go." That was it. Clunk.

That evening I watched the six o'clock news. There wasn't any mention of the Brown case. Not a hint about what we had been working on. So I hung around the house until about nine o'clock, when Don came by to take Mom out for a drink, and naturally I asked him what was going on.

"Maybe," he said mysteriously, "you'd better talk to Barbara."

The next day I tried to get her on the phone. Barbara was busy in the editing room, I was told, but she'd get back to me. I waited for hours by the phone, but it never rang. I tried her again and was told she was out covering a strike. So I left another message. She didn't return that one either.

This was getting me nowhere. Finally, I called Bill. "I feel as if everybody's avoiding me. Will *you* tell me what's happening?"

"Paul just quit."

"Quit!"

"Yeah. They're looking for a new assignment editor. Unless," he added lightly, "I can convince them I'm not too green to take it over. But it's all up in the air; I'm not even sure if I'm staying on."

I was getting tired of asking the same question. "Does this have anything to do with what we were working on?"

"That I couldn't tell you. Paul doesn't talk about these things. He just says he couldn't take their 'philosophical differences about what is news and what isn't.' Anyway, the place is in a bit of an upheaval. Dave and

I are splitting Paul's work temporarily . . . which means I'm pulling most of the weight by myself.''

"Barbara isn't answering my calls.''

"Well, she's pretty harried.''

"You mean," I said hopefully, "because she's going on her regular stories and the Brown case, too?''

"You're not going to let me off the hook, are you, Caroline?''

"That's right. I'm not.''

"She's not going out on Brown anymore. It's been called off.''

"*Why*?''

"Dave . . .'' He sighed. ''. . . says we're short-handed here as it is. We haven't got the time to spare. And he's got a point.''

"But that's not the real reason!" I stormed. "It isn't, is it?''

"You're asking me things I can't answer because I don't know.''

"Do you *want* to know, Bill?''

"Take care of yourself. 'Bye.'' The phone went dead.

I was beside myself—so worked up I couldn't stand it anymore. "I've got to see Barbara right now!" I shouted aloud. "Right now!" But the phone suddenly rang. Maybe it's her! I thought—and snapped it up.

"It's me. . . .''

"Helen!''

"I'm home again," she said breathlessly. "And we just have to talk. Can I see you right away?''

"Helen, I want to. I want to very much. But I have to go down to the newsroom first. . . .''

"It's the same thing again!" she shouted. "It never

changes.'' She slammed the phone down so hard my ears rang.

Now I didn't know what to do. I felt as if I was being ripped in half from two directions. I ran out of the house, then ran right back in again and called Helen.

There was no answer. I guess she didn't want to talk to a friend like me right then.

When I got out on the street again, I jumped on my bike and rode off. The only thing is that at that moment I didn't have the slightest idea where I was headed— whether to Helen's or Channel 12. Either way I had to go up to the next set of traffic lights before turning one direction or the other. I was trusting something that was not my head to make the choice for me at the last moment. Pedaling fast, I came up to the light and went into a glide—

Decision time!

A taxi made up my mind for me, by cutting me off on the left. I swung around to the right, headed for the station.

It was a long haul to get there. Tired and sweating as I was, I barreled through the newsroom door.

''Bill?''

As he looked up from the assignment desk, a satisfied little smile came on his face. It was just as if he had *expected* me to show up.

''Where's Barbara?''

''I really don't know,'' he said pretty loudly—but at the same time nodded meaningfully in the direction of Dave Hammersmith's office.

I rushed up to the door but then I thought the better of it and suddenly stopped. Barbara isn't going anywhere, I told myself. She has to come out. And after awhile, she did.

Like Bill, she too didn't seem completely surprised at finding me there. "You look perfectly furious with me, Caroline."

"You're not working on it anymore, are you?"

"No, I'm not. In fact, I'm busy on something else now. And I'm in a hurry. But come along with me and we'll talk."

"All right."

We walked outside quickly and climbed into her car. "You're not taking Don along?"

"Just something I have to look up at the Hall of Records before it closes." She gave me a little smile. "Have to do it myself these days if I want it done right. I don't trust our new intern as much as I did you."

All that was meant as a peace gesture, but I batted the line right back at her. "And I trusted you, too, Barbara."

There was a long pause. "Sorry to disappoint you, then."

"At least," I ranted on, "Paul *quit* when they wouldn't let him go with the story!"

"Paul didn't have a contract," she answered slowly and evenly. "Also, I don't know exactly why he did quit."

"I don't believe that."

"Well, it's entirely up to you. Although I am sorry you think of me as a fallen angel." She turned a look of her own on me. "I never asked you to put me on that pedestal in the first place." She paused. "Was there never someone *you* disappointed though you couldn't help it?"

She had stung me with visions of Helen . . . and

perhaps even of how I had turned off to my dad. It made my face burn; I didn't like it. There's a whole world of difference, I told myself, between this and what happened between me and my friends and family. A *human life* is at stake here!

"Barbara, if the only reason you stopped was because you're needed on other stories, then why didn't you keep digging and searching on your *own* time?"

"Did I say that's what it was?"

"You *admit* there was another reason? What was it? Did Hammersmith stop you because Benjamin Sorell had something to do with this station?"

". . . Dave did pull me off the story. But when you work with people, you can't go around churning inside because you think that all their motives are the worst they could possibly be. That's not the way to lead your daily life, Caroline. I have to accept the fact that the person in charge here did not feel there was enough to go on. He said that any connection of the station to Sorell and Amos Walgren had nothing to do with it. Killing the story was a news judgment and a legal judgment. A decision had to be made about how much time, effort, and money they could keep putting into this. I may not have agreed with that decision, but I had to accept it."

"If you didn't agree with it, then why didn't you take what you have somewhere else? Give it to Channel 8 so *they* can do something about it?"

"That would be unethical."

"Unethical!" I exploded. "Isn't it more unethical to leave Willy Brown in jail for life—or on his way to an execution?"

"We can argue that—but the videotapes are not my property. They belong to the station."

"The medical records weren't our property either, but we were ready to use them."

"Professionally, Caroline, I couldn't do what you're asking. I'd be thrown out of the business."

"So would my mother from hers if they ever find out what she did!"

She pulled the car over to a curb. "Perhaps we'd better bring this to an end."

I gazed around. "This doesn't look like the Hall of Records to me."

"No, but I think we've said enough to each other. Can you get home from here?" There was a tremor in her voice.

"I have to go back for my bike."

"I'll ask Don to drop it off for you."

"Okay." I opened the door.

"Well, good-bye, Caroline."

I huskily whispered, "Good-bye," and rushed away. I hadn't wanted to end things like this.

I didn't go straight to my house. I felt miserable and I wanted to do something about it.

Helen was at home when I rang her doorbell, but she came to the upstairs window instead. "What do *you* want?"

"What do you think I want?"

She disappeared and finally showed up at the front door, which she held open for me as if I were a leper she was stuck with having to let pass. "Okay . . . come on in."

I held my ground. "No, I don't want to go inside. I want to walk."

"So walk!" She stepped back as if she were going to slam the door on me.

"I want you to walk with me."

"What is this? A test of power?"

"No . . . I'm just feeling restless." Then I shouted, "You know me—I get *restless*! I am not *perfect*!"

"You're not perfect? That's big news. . . . Okay— wait a minute. I'll get my sandals."

She came out a moment later—barefoot.

"I thought you wanted your sandals."

"Changed my mind. I'm not perfect either. Where do you want to walk?"

"I don't care."

"So why don't we go around the block then? That will be symbolic. You and I have been going in circles anyway."

"Must you make these comments?"

"Yes!" she cried hotly as we started to walk. "That way I won't feel so humiliated because I need you for my friend!"

"In that case, I don't know what your problem is— because I *am* your friend!" I stopped and looked at her. "I am, Helen, I really am."

"Well you don't always show it!" There were tears in her eyes.

"Sometimes . . . I can't. But I'm sorry if I let you down. I mean that. I'm very sorry."

She took a deep breath and said, "Okay. Let's forget it."

"You're sure?"

"Yes, I'm sure."

Only she sort of grumbled it. Se we walked in an

awkward silence all the way around the block, then started around it again.

"That business with Moe Stern was really dumb," she grimly said at last.

"Are you honestly over it?"

"No—but I've already had my fit. What's next after that except to be philosophical?"

"And what does your philosophy say?"

"That the business with Moe Stern was really dumb. Another circle, okay?"

"Oh Helen! I don't want things to be bad between us. You are my friend. And I need you and I love you."

"As much as you need Barbara Richie?"

"Why do you even ask that?"

"I'm asking."

"Yes! And more. But that's different from the way I care about you—and I don't feel it's right to compare. I don't want to apologize for caring about Barbara. What I do want to apologize for is . . . not being there when you needed me."

Then Helen surprised me. She came out of herself and said, "Look, you were just caught up in something very important to you—and to someone else, too. I only wish I had something like that. . . . So what are we down to? Each other, right?"

"Yeah, right."

"Well," she said, giving me a long look, "that sounds pretty good to me."

"Me too."

Then we both cried a little, and walked around the block until we felt a lot better.

*   *   *

It was still my mother's vacation time, but when I got home she was out keeping a hairdressing appointment. The clock said two minutes to six. Out of habit, I guess, I put on the Channel 12 news.

I didn't expect anything glorious, though, and the show lived up to my nonexpectations. As usual, Blake was charming and Barbara was charming, but I couldn't help feeling that anyone could have done the same job of reeling off the news that was handed to them. Before the broadcast was even over, I turned off the set, wondering if what I really wanted out of life was to be a television journalist.

The phone rang, and I sort of glumly picked it up.

"Hi, Caroline."

"Paul!"

"I got the feeling you're not going to give up on this, are you?"

"Nope."

"Well, you might think of driving up around the Millford area in Weston County, across the river. You know where that is?"

"I think so. Why?"

"There are some migrant farm workers in around there. It's just a thought, but you might check it out."

"Thanks, Paul! Could you come along with me?"

"Thanks for asking, Caroline, but I'm out of the business. I've had enough, but that doesn't mean I can't give you some help."

"I don't understand, Paul. Why did you quit? I knew Barbara was threatening to walk away from it all, but I never thought you'd quit. I thought giving the public the news was your life?"

"Well, Caroline, sometimes what you think the public should know and what they actually end up knowing are two different things. That discrepancy was getting to be too big a pill for me to swallow."

I didn't know what to say. I felt confused and strangely relieved for Paul.

"But don't get me wrong," he said. "Dave Hammersmith isn't as bad a guy as you think. He's got to balance the pressures from both directions, and it isn't easy. Anyway, I don't want to scare you, but one way or another Ben Sorell's got to know by now what's been going on. If he did kill his wife, he's got a lot to protect. So be extra careful out there, just to please your old assignment editor."

"I will. I promise."

"Good luck."

As I hung up I felt as if I'd already had some good luck. I was back in action!

Chapter 20

As MY MOTHER, Helen, and I drove out toward Millford, I felt I had to tell her about Paul's warning. She wasn't overjoyed to hear it, naturally, but she didn't insist on turning back or making a big noise about it. She just quietly made a detour to a store and came out of it with a can of Mace.

We spent most of the day getting shrugs and shakes of the heads, but then, on the last farm we came to, someone took us aside to say that she knew a George Blackwell. She described him as a big man, about fifty, and graying. Only she had no idea where we could look for him.

"Well," I said as we drove off for home, "at least we know he exists!"

"This is so exciting!" Helen exclaimed the next day as we turned off an empty country road with a broken signpost and on to one that didn't have any signpost at all.

We had re-established our friendship, and Helen had once and for all given up men—until of course the next guy who smiled at her came along. So she had decided to come along and see what I'd been up to for the summer.

"The word is *aggravating*," my mother said.

Still *more* of nothing. And by now we were all starving as well. Just ahead we spotted a few shacks just off the road. The place had a totally deserted look, but someone had to be living there.

"Listen you two," my mother said, "I don't want any arguments. I'm going in by myself. Helen, you know how to drive away. So get behind the wheel."

I kept telling myself that I ought to go after her as she disappeared among the shacks. There are times, though, when you don't argue with my mother.

She came back ten minutes later saying, "They were very suspicious of me. As usual no one was willing to tell me what they know."

Helen climbed into the rear seat, my mother turned the car back around, and we headed onto the road.

"Mom, did you remember to ask about George Blackwell?"

"Of course I asked. That's why we're here, right?"

"Sorry. I can only blame it on my stomach."

"We will eat. I promise you we will eat."

"Did either of you see a car in that place?" Helen asked all of a sudden.

I shook my head and my mother said no.

"Neither did I, but there's one behind us now. And I don't know where else it could have come from."

I looked around. Except for being very dusty, it was an ordinary-looking car.

"I certainly didn't see that car back there," my mother said.

The road continued on to an intersection with a wider road. It was our best shot for finding someplace to eat. We turned onto it.

"That car's making the same turn, Mrs. Burns."

"There aren't many options," my mother said.

About two miles farther on we spotted a small diner coming up on the left, and my mother signaled the turn.

Helen pointed behind her. "Look! That car's turning, too."

"Restaurants would go out of business if more than one car didn't, my dear."

"Mom," I said quickly as we swung into the lot, "pull out again. Don't stop."

"Why?"

"Just please do it. I want to see something!"

"And I thought you were starved," she answered, making a wide sweep that took us back across the road.

"It *is* following us!" Helen cried. The car behind us had done the same thing.

"So now what?" Mom was trying to keep her calm.

"Keep going," I said.

"Look for a police car!" Helen shouted.

"Mom, can't you go faster?"

"I am not going to get into the kind of chase you see in the movies! I will not wreck this car."

"Mrs. Burns, you've got to! It's catching up to us!"

"I'll go a little faster, but that's it."

We speeded up to fifty-five. "Faster," I pleaded when the other car picked up speed, too.

"I am not going over the legal limit."

"So we'll get a ticket!" I screamed. "That's what we want! We *want* the cops!"

"The biggest danger we all face is if I don't drive safely. Stop making me nervous."

"I can't believe this is happening to me!" Helen kept repeating, but she seemed to to be enjoying the excitement. My mother and I on the other hand were nearing panic.

"Hold on!" My mom gave a twist to the wheel, sending it into a spin that was straight out of the movies.

There was a highway overpass ahead, and we shot up the narrow, curving ramp leading to it. "Mom!" I yelled as a Do Not Enter sign whizzed by. "It's the wrong way!"

"Too late! I can't stop now!" She blasted the horn flat out and kept going.

"We'll all be killed!" Helen shrieked with a grin.

"We will if you don't stop screaming in my ears!"

As our car careened onto the roadway, we could see the other car tearing right on up after us. We drove along like this for a while and, over our blaring horn, my mother suddenly let fly a bunch of words I never thought she knew.

"Mrs. Burns, that car's getting closer!"

"I'm going as fast as I can."

There was a sign coming up, and I pointed. "Get off at that exit."

"Why?"

"It goes back to town."

"How do you know?"

"I know."

We swung off onto another ramp and, when we came roaring to the bottom, jumped the red light.

So did the other car.

We blasted along, probably doing everything other than what we should have been doing to find a police station—and kept going until familiar places showed up. Like frightened homing pigeons, we were on our own street. And there was the house!

We jumped out of the car, ran for the house, fumbled for keys, and got inside—just as that other car came barreling to a stop behind us. We slammed the door and secured the chain on it.

We heard the other car's door slam shut . . . and then footsteps. "Mom," I whispered, "get out your Mace."

As we stood there, shuddering with fear, there were footsteps on the wooden porch. Then a knocking at the door. We didn't move.

Why doesn't whoever it is just break in? I thought. And I began edging toward the door. "We have a loaded gun," I called. "Who are you? Why are you chasing us?"

"My name is George Blackwell."

I turned to my mother. "How . . . how do we know that?" she asked loudly.

"I'm Willy's friend. People say you looking all over for me. I want to help."

"If that's true," I asked suspiciously, "why did you wait this long to do something about it?"

"I'm not proud of myself. What happened to Willy has been on my conscience all the time. Every minute. But I've been so afraid . . ."

"That doesn't explain," called my mother, "why you followed us just now."

"Because . . . because when you came to my door—right up to where I was hiding—then I realized that Ben

Sorell and his friends could sure find me, too! So we've got to help each other!''

"Wait a minute,'' I said, and slipping to the window, carefully peeked out from between the slats of the Venetian blinds. I saw a black man with graying hair. "Mom, I think it is him.''

We were all shaking, but we let George Blackwell in.

Chapter 21

"HELLO, BILL," I SAID twenty minutes later when he answered the phone. "Guess what?"

"You've come up with George Blackwell."

"How did *you* know?"

"Just had a hunch about you. What've you got?"

"Him at my house—now."

"Does he back up Willy Brown's story?"

"Yep!"

"All the way?"

"Yep."

"Did you get his story down on tape, just in case he wants to back out of it?"

"Got it on a cassette right in my hand. Now let me ask *you* something."

"Okay."

"Will Dave Hammersmith go with this story *right now*—I mean tonight and one hundred percent—or do I call Channel 8 instead and give it to them? And if I do, I'll let them know about all the other stuff you people have been sitting on."

"Hold on . . ." He went off the line and came back a couple of minutes later. "No problem."

"What does that mean, Bill?"

"If it's what you say it is, we'll go with it big, even if we have to pre-empt time and put on a special. That suit you?"

"Sounds all right. Tell Barbara to hurry up, because Mr. Blackwell is very, very nervous."

"Uh . . . yeah . . ."

"We're *all* nervous, Bill," I added. "So don't waste any time."

We went into the kitchen where Mom was trying to keep Mr. Blackwell occupied by serving him a sandwich and making conversation. "What I don't understand," she asked, "is why you didn't just leave the state if you were so afraid after you heard about your friend's arrest? Why did you stay so close?"

Mr. Blackwell scratched his head. "Well, I thought about that and the only thing I came up with was that if I had gone back to Louisiana, I would be more upset and confused than I am now. I guess I wanted to give my *conscience* a chance to do the right thing even though my *body* wanted to do the safe thing."

My mother had made some food for the rest of us, too, and I sat down at the table, starved. About ten minutes into the meal, we heard a car stop outside.

They've certainly made it fast, I told myself, going to the front porch window. A black car stood along the curb with its motor still running and two men inside.

Only one got out. He looked up and down the empty block, then started for the house.

"Mother!" I cried in a heavy whisper.

She rushed in from the kitchen. "What is it?"

"They're not from the station!"

"Oh, Lord," said George Blackwell, coming in right behind her with Helen. "I *knew* they'd come to kill me! They're goin' to kill us all!"

Just then the doorbell rang. Mom motioned me not to answer and ran off.

I couldn't speak. Standing there silently, we began to hear a jiggling noise. The lock was starting to turn.

"The chain is off!" Helen gasped under her breath and, although she was trembling, darted past me to the door and slid the chain on.

The door opened against it. I stood there frozen to the spot. Through the growing space I could see the man pressing on it with his shoulder. He was testing the chain. He drew back as if getting ready to snap it off in one big push.

Then all at once, the man and my mother rushed for the door at the same time. She got to it a split second before he did, shoved the Mace can up to it, and let loose into his face. He reeled back, screaming. My mother slammed the door hard and sagged against the wall.

"There's another one!" I gasped, and rushed to the window. The man on the porch was flailing around, but the one who'd been behind the wheel of the car was already out of it and heading for us. Reaching the bottom porch step, he spotted me and drew a gun from his jacket. I raced to the little sewing table and pulled out the long scissors.

"Put that down!" my mother demanded.

"But he's got a gun!"

Mr. Blackwell snatched the scissors from my hands. "Go on," he whispered quickly to all of us. "You get out the back and I'll stop 'em."

Why none of us moved, I'll never know. Maybe there really wasn't enough time. Or maybe we couldn't leave him there. It could even be that we all sensed that something else had happened. Everything had fallen silent on the other side of the door.

Then there were footsteps hurrying away. . . .

We heard the car drive off, and—only seconds later— another arriving. I heard a voice I recognized.

"It's Don!"

I would have run to the door if there had been anything left in my knees but Jell-O. Instead, I practically crawled over, opened it, and saw him lifting his photographer's equipment out of the van.

I waited for Barbara to climb out of the van. I wanted to see her expression. I wanted her to know what I had accomplished.

But it was Blake Thomas who stepped out from the van's passenger side. And *he* looked absolutely thrilled! Watching him walk toward me, all my expectations—my excitement—shifted into anger. "What are *you* doing here instead of Barbara?"

"Not Blake's fault," called Don, coming up behind him, lugging everything by himself. "Bill was afraid to tell you that Barbara was in New York, meeting with the network biggies—and risk losing this story. Looks like she may have her shot after all."

"What?"

"Network wants a replacement for 'Hello U.S.A.' and Barbara's got it," Don replied.

"Caroline!" my mother said from behind me. "Why are we standing here talking about Barbara Richie? Let's get to the matter at hand. Those two men."

"What are you talking about?" Don asked.

"Two men!" She pointed down the road. "Didn't you see them drive away?"

"No. Who?"

"How do I know? They were hoodlums. They tried to break the door in. One of them had a gun!" She headed back inside. "I'm going to call the police."

Blake's smile stiffened and he raced in after her, yelling, "No! Wait! Don't! Please don't!"

"And why shouldn't I?" I heard my mother yell back. "Is there something wrong with the city's police force, too?"

"Mrs. Burns, that's not it. Please listen. If you call them now, someone there will tip off our competition. When Channel 8 hears about this, they'll be down here in no time and we'll lose our scoop!"

"Mom—" I said.

"I don't understand you people." She sighed and put down the phone.

I have to admit that once Blake Thomas set to work he really was very good. First, off he went into the kitchen to calm down Mr. Blackwell, who had good reason to worry that those men would come after him again.

"Your best insurance against that, Mr. Blackwell, is for us to get your story down on tape and put it on the air right away. That's what they wanted to stop."

While Don checked the house for the best lighting,

Blake sat himself down in the living room to play back the interview I'd recorded on my cassette, and made a few notes. "You did some job here, Caroline," he told me at last.

"Thank you." I was beginning to like him better all the time.

The interview with George Blackwell went just fine. It sounded terrific. After it was over Blake shook hands with all of us and complimented me again.

As the three men were leaving together, my mother followed them to the porch and drew Don aside. I had wanted to speak to him as well as overhear their conversation. "Does this mean," my mother asked, "that you'll be leaving here for New York, too—to be working with her?"

"I don't really know. Let's take it as it comes."

"But you could get that offer?"

"Yes, I could."

"Then what? Will you go?"

Don didn't answer her directly. "Look at it this way. They also have nursing jobs in New York City, don't they?"

"That would be quite a change for me . . . and Caroline."

"Well . . . like I said." He smiled at her.

"Yes, like you said." She smiled back.

"Hey, Don!" Blake called. "We've got a lot to do between now and the broadcast!"

"Coming."

I followed him down the stairs. "Tell me why they're letting Barbara go?"

"Dave said they finally realized it made no sense to hold someone who really resented being there."

"They could have thought of that a long time ago," I called as he walked away. "What was the *real* reason, Don?"

He stopped the van and took awhile to answer. My guess is that the network was in a bind, without a morning anchorwoman. So they turned the thumbscrews on the boys at Channel 12. Couldn't have happened to a bunch of nicer guys!"

He drove off leaving me wondering whether he had said that just make me feel better—or that was the true and only reason Barbara had been given the chance to live out her dream. . . .

Chapter 22

FOR MORE THAN an hour there had been break-in announcements over the regular shows to stay tuned for an important special report during the six o'clock news. It was a real build-up—and now, as we sat watching the set, the broadcast finally came on.

It opened on Blake Thomas sitting alone at the anchor desk. "There has been a startling development in the Willy Brown case. He is the farm worker who was convicted last month of the brutal murder of Agnes Sorell. He may not have been the murderer at all. He may have been the Good Samaritan who rushed to her rescue. A new witness has come out of hiding to give an exclusive interview to Channel 12. Stay with us. More after this. . . ."

My mother pressed the remote control in her hand, shutting off a commercial, and turned to me. "Well, you did it, Caroline. Congratulations.'' She kissed me on the cheek.

"*We* did it, Mom."

"Yes, but are you happy now?"

"Nobody's freed him yet."

"That part of it is out of our hands."

Which was exactly it, I guess. There would be no more rushing around tracking down leads. No more feeling as if I was still a broadcast journalist and that the Willy Brown story was my baby. It had gone out over the airwaves without me. All I could do now was stay at home like a doting mother and wait to see what happened next.

I took another glance at my own mother calmly sitting beside me on the sofa, looking so much like anybody else. Never in a million years could I have imagined that she would actually consider changing her whole life—and mine—by going off to New York City with a man she'd only just met a few weeks before. But then, who would have expected her to play Sherlock Holmes of the medical records room or to go Macing gunmen?

The rapid squeak of our rocking chair made me look at Helen. She was more excited for me than even I was. "Start the sound, Mrs. Burns! It's on again!"

Back at his anchor desk, Blake recited a short lead-in. "This afternoon, our reporter was called to an address which we will not at this time disclose—"

"What!" Helen jumped out of her rocker. "That's the most stupid thing I ever heard. Sorell already knows where it is!"

"We can't hear him," my mother said.

"Helen, shut up! They don't want Channel 8 here, that's all."

"And met with a man," Blake was continuing, "who identified himself as George Blackwell, a friend of Brown's."

By now, Mr. Blackwell was being shown on tape, sitting in our kitchen, talking to Blake.

"About three years ago, I used to work for Mr. Sorell on his farm, so I know him pretty good. Willy, he never met the man. And he didn't want to go by himself to ask for a week off. His sister was very sick down in Virginia. They were very close. So he asked me to go with him because he heard Mr. Sorell was a *hard* man. Willy couldn't afford to be fired. So we went there together. . . ."

"How did you go?"

"Oh, we walked from the farm to the town . . . about two miles. And when we got to the front of the house, we heard Mrs. Sorell. She was screaming. But I told Willy that I wasn't going in there. He said, 'Well, that woman is in trouble.' I still said I wasn't going in. I warned him, but he went in anyways. I just took off. I'm not proud of it, but that's the way it was."

"Did you see anyone come out of the house?"

"No, I heard a sound around the back, but I didn't see anyone. I didn't stay for that! I just took off."

"Then why did you think that it was Mr. Sorell who was hurting her?"

". . . I guess I'd heard something about that stuff going on before."

"From whom?"

"Oh, that I don't remember."

"But you do remember that Willy Brown ran into the

house only *after* you heard Agnes Sorell screaming and
pleading with someone?''

"Oh, yes! Oh, yes! Willy went in to help!''

The scene switched back to Blake at the anchor desk.
"Blackwell said he went into hiding after he heard of
the Brown arrest. He claims that he was afraid to go to
the Ridgewood Park police because . . .''

Blackwell came on again in our living room saying,
"That police chief is a long-time friend of Mr. Sorell's.''

"How do you know?''

"Oh, they used to come out to the farm with some
other men.''

"Do you know who or why?''

He shook his head. "I don't know for sure. But
they were friendly.''

Now Blake was on—at the anchor desk. "Tomorrow
there will be a further report on this developing situation.
Stay with us for the rest of the evening news after this
commercial message.''

"I don't understand!'' Helen cried out. "What happened to the rest of it—those other interviews?''

"Show biz.'' I was trying to sound like an old pro.

"Mrs. Burns, I bet I know the real reason that reporter begged you not to call the police to come here.''

"What's that?''

"To keep Caroline from getting any credit. He never
mentioned her name on the broadcast!''

Of course I knew he hadn't, but I didn't want to feel
that the main reason I had worked so hard was to get a
lot of applause. Once she put it into words, I have to
say that I did feel a pang.

The next day, the local newspaper picked up the
story. And even Channel 8 said something, during its

morning news briefs, about the possibility of there being some new evidence in the case. But we—I mean, Channel 12—still had the ball!

Blake came on that evening with a statement that Barbara Richie had left Channel 12. He gave her a sincere-sounding send-off, then went into the next special report, her interview with Jim Timmerman.

Actually, a lot of it had been edited. It was much shorter. Still, all the main things came out—the years of Agnes Sorell's being battered around by her husband . . . the police doing nothing about it when Mr. Timmerman called them . . . his attempts to help Willy Brown by meeting with the lawyer . . . and then the silent threats. . . .

I wasn't mentioned in this interview either. Barbara wasn't even in it, and you didn't hear her either. To someone who didn't know—and with all that back and forth to the anchor desk—it looked as if Blake had been the one who interviewed Timmerman. I had to work very hard not to become upset. Even my mother looked concerned.

Chapter 23

I'M NOT GOING to go into everything now that happened over the next couple of weeks. But one thing came out right after another. That lawyer, Giezel, didn't even wait for the interview we had taped with him to be shown on the next broadcast. He went straight to the district attorney's office and offered to "cooperate" in exchange for not going to jail. By now, too, the competition—and even channels and newspapers from other areas—were working hard to get into the act. Pushed from everywhere at once, the DA gave in and held a short news conference that went on TV.

By now my mother was back on her night shift. Helen and I hung together, glued to the living room set, waiting for new things to happen. The truth is, she was more stuck than I was. Of course, I wanted desperately for everything to come out right for Willy Brown. But there was something in me that was turning bitter—and

I especially felt it every time the Channel 12 news came on.

Early the next morning Helen burst into the house shouting, "Let's go!"

"Quiet!" I said, "my mother's still sleeping."

"Then get her up! Haven't you heard the announcement?"

"What announcement?"

"The judge is letting Willy Brown go free today at ten o'clock."

"You . . . you mean it?"

"Yes—and everybody's going to be there! So let those guys at Channel 12 just *try* to keep you out of the news when Brown sees you as he's coming back down the courthouse steps!"

I was still feeling funny about it all when the three of us drove downtown and parked behind the courthouse. Part of the reason, I suspect, was that my mother was so silent along the way.

Photographers and reporters were already gathered on the steps—and soon the place became thick with them. They hadn't just come from nearby stations and papers. The Associated Press and the networks had sent their own people down, and there were others from all over the place.

This was suddenly more than a local story. There was political coverup, a framed man, and another man—a powerful one—whom everyone believed was guilty, but nobody could be sure would be brought to trial to pay for it. There was also the issue it raised, if anyone was interested, about what it really took to make sure that there was liberty and *justice* for all.

Anyway, that's how I intended to write about it for my school newpaper. Meanwhile, we waited for Willy Brown to come out. Two-thirty came and went . . . two-forty . . . two-fifty . . . three. Then all at once, there was a flurry at the courthouse entrance. The wide doors pushed open and Willy Brown appeared at the top of the stairs with George Blackwell at his side.

The reporters and cameramen went to work.

But Willy Brown just stared back at them with an expression on his face that gave me a jab in the heart. It was a look that said to me he didn't know whether all this was any more real than the other part of what had happened to him—the nightmare. Was it really over? Bewilderment and pain still shone in those eyes.

I wanted to stand in front of him and say something that would make him realize that he was free, that it was over . . . that he was safe.

"Come on," I suddenly said. "Let's get out of here."

Helen glared at me. "What are you talking about? You have to stay till he comes down the steps."

"No!" I cried.

"What?"

My mother took us both by the arm. "Helen, don't argue with her. Let's go."

But Helen did argue—all the way home. "I don't understand you at all. You're supposed to be a reporter. You're supposed to get the story, to be there when the news is made."

"There was no reason for me to be there, Helen, except to collect a reward."

My mother couldn't stay to watch the six o'clock

news with us. But before she left for work, she took my hands in hers. "About that reward," she said softly.

"I don't expect one," I said too quickly.

"Yes, you do, and you need it."

"Watching him be freed is enough."

"No, it's not quite enough."

Later on, Helen and I sat in front of the TV and watched Willy Brown come down the courthouse stairs. With every step he took, the nightmare seemed to lift, his eyes grew brighter, and by the time he reached the place where I had been standing, he was glowing.

"See, Caroline, you should have waited."

"What for? I'm watching it now." I was glowing more than Willy at that moment. I knew I had gotten my reward.